RECKLESS
WEEKEND

RECKLESS BEAT   BOOK 2.5
EDEN SUMMERS

DEDICATION

To all the blessings in my life. My husband that gives me a reason to write romance. My kids who test my mental stability but continuously make me smile. My friends who never, ever quit encouraging me. And the music that inspires the stories of the Reckless Beat men.

Thank you to all those who continue to support my writing. I hope you enjoy the Reckless Weekend ride.

CHAPTER 1

"**R**ELAX, ALLIE. LET ME TAKE THE STRESS AWAY."

Alana whimpered at Mitchell's softly spoken words, and the brush of his lips against her naked collarbone. She wanted to melt into the deliciousness of his touch. To sink into his masculine scent and be thoroughly pleasured. It wouldn't happen, though. The pressure of the wedding had wound her body tight. There was also the anxiety that came from her mother's presence, the bachelorette party that brought them to Vegas, and the dreaded honeymoon. Their romantic trip away had become the bane of her existence.

"You're so tense." He spoke in a gravel-rich tone, while one calloused hand massaged her shoulder.

She let out a heavy breath. "I can't help it." Really, she couldn't. She'd been riding the epinephrine train too long to disembark temporarily to relax.

He guided her to the bed, and she fell back onto the luxurious hotel mattress, allowing her fiancé to spread her knees and move between them. He leaned into her, his naked body still wet from the shower, his muscles glistening. Not a day went by that she wasn't thankful for the changes he brought to her life.

"God, you smell good," he purred, the rough stubble of his jaw grazing her inner thigh. He leaned on his elbows, the edge of his lips tilting in a wicked grin as his gaze found her heat. "I've been trying to get you alone all day."

Alana sighed, wishing arousal would take hold. "I'm sorry, but I told you, I've got too much on my mind to enjoy this right now."

He climbed higher, the warmth of his chest settling between her bare legs, the heat of his breath tickling her skin. "Sounds like a challenge." He lowered his face, his lips hovering a whisper away from her sex. Tempting. Teasing. "You've done so much work for this wedding. Let me do a little something for you." He pressed his mouth to her pussy, separating her folds with a gentle stroke of his tongue before retreating. "What do you think, Allie? Can I play for a little while? Maybe take the edge off."

Her core clenched, sparking to life with tingles that spread all the way through her stomach, tightening her nipples.

"This isn't going to be as challenging as I thought." He chuckled, and swiped her slit with his tongue. His arms wrapped around her thighs, holding her tight as his mouth sank further, becoming more demanding with every brush of his lips.

She squirmed, searching for deeper penetration, more friction. Her fingers ran through his chin-length hair and held him close. That's when her mind regained control, assailing her with questions she didn't want to answer. How would Mitchell do his hair for the wedding? Did he plan to get it styled? Cut? Would he shave? Did he realize the wedding photos would be displayed in magazines, on the television, and all over the Internet?

"I've lost you again, haven't I?" He placed a gentle kiss on her mound.

She whimpered. This was so unfair. She had the most gorgeous rock star between her thighs, his sole focus on *her* pleasure, and still she couldn't concentrate.

Two fingers teased her entrance, nudging, regaining her attention. She shuddered with her body's need for more, and moaned when his mouth lowered to her clit, sucking, making it throb.

"That feels good," she panted, releasing his hair. She skimmed her hands over her stomach, cupping her breasts and tweaking her now aching nipples.

His fingers slid deeper, twisting, pulsing, building her arousal until her thoughts were consumed with her impending climax. She needed this release. She needed the short moment of earth shattering bliss to get her through the coming days. Most of all, she needed him. Mitchell always soothed her.

"I want to touch you," she whispered. The hardness of his body comforted her, lessening the harsh doubts and worries that assailed her. In these moments, when the two of them were caught in the web of lust and passion, nothing else mattered. It was the only thing that cleared her mind, yet she'd been too anxious lately to bother trying.

Mitchell rose, resting his weight on his hands, penetrating her with his hazel stare. "Do I have your full attention?" He leaned down to lick a trail along her stomach, stopping when he reached her nipple. He sucked the hardened flesh into his mouth, flicking it with his tongue, before releasing it with a pop. "Have you stopped thinking enough for me to enjoy this pretty little body of yours?"

She nodded, and rose to her elbows, making him retreat onto his haunches. "I want to touch you."

He growled, cupping the back of her neck and pulling her forward for a deep kiss. Their tongues stroked, the slight taste of her own pleasure entering her mouth. She ran her hands down his body, from his shoulders, over the taut muscles of his stomach, to grip his thick erection.

"Stroke me," he begged against her lips. "Hard."

Nothing was more empowering than having Mitchell at her mercy. But instead of complying, she moved onto all fours, and rested her lips against the head of his cock. His hands tangled in her loose hair, and he moaned as she licked the pre-cum beading his slit.

He tugged at her hair, pulling her forward, encouraging her to take him deeper. "Christ, Allie, you make me so fuckin' hard."

She rested a hand against his thigh for stability, and opened her lips wider, sucking him into her mouth. Her tongue worked around his cock head, down the ridge, while she savored the scent of soap and man. When her free hand brushed the tightness of his sac, he jerked forward, the involuntary movement making her smile.

"Please, baby. Please, let me fuck your mouth."

She responded by loosening her suction and sliding her lips down to the base of his shaft, delighting in the guttural moan that followed.

He thrust into her with short, sharp jolts. "Look at me." He cupped her cheeks, and she stared up at his glazed eyes. "You're a dream, you know that? A beautiful, sexy, entirely perfect dream. I can't wait until you're mine forever."

Alana winced at the wedding reminder and broke eye contact, not wanting to hinder his bliss. There was too much to organize in so little time—the finishing touches to the seating plan, organizing the out-of-town guests with airport transfers, and then there was the honeymoon. The damn vacation was sending her on a quick slide into a nervous breakdown.

"Hey." His hands circled her neck, demanding her attention, making her shiver from his dominance. "Come back to me." He fell from her mouth and encouraged her to straighten, bringing them chest to chest. His arm curled around her waist as he sat back on his haunches and dragged her body with him.

She straddled his lap and stared into his eyes, wishing he would take her stress away. The wedding had to be perfect. The world would be judging him—them—and creating a fairytale day was the one thing she could give him for everything he'd ever done for her. He'd shown her a life outside of her sheltered upbringing. He'd created a job that enabled them to be together. He'd paid for a wedding fit for a queen, not once bothering to worry about the expense.

In return, she gave her love in spades, only it didn't seem enough. She wanted to give him one special day that would show the world how much they meant to each other. She needed to convince his fans she was worthy. And maybe, deep down, she still needed to prove it to herself, too.

The head of his shaft nudged her entrance, sliding through her slick arousal, breaking her train of thought. He surged forward, penetrating her in one hard thrust, tearing a scream of delight from her throat.

"That's my girl," he cooed, leaning in to nip the side of her jaw with his teeth.

She arched her back, grinding her pelvis against him, searching for friction against her clit. His mouth moved lower, finding her breast, licking, sucking, making her body hotter, her mind blank.

"Faster," she pleaded.

The bed squeaked with his next thrust, and they moaned in unison. She straightened, taking his lips with force, her tongue brushing his. They battled with their mouths, their bodies, and hands. Her fingers scoured his back, and he let out a hiss that temporarily broke the kiss, before slamming his lips back down on hers with more ferocity.

It felt good to drift away, to ignore the world, the future, and her never-ending to-do list, and simply enjoy. Her body vibrated, her blood boiled, and with each forceful thrust of his hips, it made her more determined to forget her troubles.

"I'm gonna make you come so hard, Allie," he growled into her mouth, their noses bumping with each upward slam of his pelvis.

She already knew he would. He always did. Yet, the promise still sent a heated shiver of anticipation through her body. He placed his pointer finger against her lips, sliding it inside to press against her tongue. Unsure what he wanted, she sucked, licking the taste of herself from his digit, until he removed it from her mouth.

His gaze narrowed, watching her with intent as he lowered his arm, gliding it around her waist, over her bottom, to tease her crack.

She shook her head at the implication, and clutched his hair to reiterate. He liked to torment her ass, to brush his fingers over the sensitive area and make her shiver. The wickedness thrilled her, but he never went any further. She wasn't sure if she wanted him to.

"Relax."

Her rampant heart did the opposite, kicking up a notch as he placed pressure on her puckered hole. "Mitchell," her voice was caught between a warning and a plea.

"Let me play for a while."

His actions changed from heated, hot and sweaty, to soft and sweet and slow. His thrusts became smooth and languorous, while his free arm held her tight around the waist. She moved against him, concentrating on the slide of his cock instead of worrying about the position of his hand. Resting her head against his shoulder, she nuzzled butterfly kisses against his neck, wishing she could read his dirty thoughts.

"Trust me?" he murmured against her ear, firmly circling his finger around her virgin entrance.

She shook her head. "Not when your hand is there."

He chuckled, nibbling her earlobe. "You'll like it."

"I lack your confidence."

He added more pressure, looming at the brink of penetration. Shame heated her cheeks at the way her pussy clamped down in needy response. Her lascivious body might have been eager to play a new game, only her mind hadn't reached that level.

"Relax against my hand."

Her spine stiffened, her muscles pulling tight. He chuckled again, long and low against her ear. He continued to sink between her thighs, building the pleasure in her core until she was grinding with force, enjoying the friction of his chest against her breasts, and relaxing into his touch.

"That's it," he murmured, nipping her neck, licking her collarbone.

His finger breached the tight band of muscle, and she gasped at the sensation. There was no pain, no discomfort, only a delicious pressure that made the warmth in her pussy increase.

"Fuck, Allie. You're so damn hot."

The thrust of his cock increased as his finger sank deeper. Delirious rapture took over. Her hips rocked, harder, faster, and she clung to him, closing her eyes as her orgasm built to the point of no return.

"I'm... I'm..." She whimpered, wanting to prolong the bliss a moment longer, even though she had no control.

Mitchell groaned in her ear, pumping with harsh strokes, ramming into her. His hair brushed her cheeks with each undulation, while one hand rested against the crack of her butt and the other wove around her back, holding the base of her neck, keeping them chest to chest.

More pressure heated her ass, while he slid another finger inside her. This time he stretched her, his movements bringing a bite of pain that added to her enjoyment. Her pussy and ass were now both deliciously full. Damn him, she was done for. Her body took over—her back arched as her walls clamped down on his cock, convulsing in wave after wave of climax. Her focus blurred and she closed her eyes, letting bliss consume her.

His demands heightened with hard, demanding thrusts, and then his groan filled the room. As he slowed, the pulse of her core faded, and she collapsed against him, falling into the heaving rise and fall of his chest. Sated and exhausted, she struggled to re-open her tired eyes, her limbs now lethargic.

"You should take a nap," Mitchell whispered into her hair, his softening cock leaving her body.

"I can't. The bachelorette party starts in little over an hour."

He leaned into her, resting her back against the mattress, and removed his fingers from her ass. She was wet between her thighs, and the tingling sensation from where his hand had just been made her cheeks heat. Sex between them was never dull. Mitchell had wanted her to experience everything life had to offer, and he'd concentrated most on the pleasures between the sheets. But anal had never been on the list. She only hoped it wouldn't create awkwardness between them—especially this close to the wedding.

Oh, who was she kidding? Mitchell would always be confident and unapologetic no matter how dirty the deed. She was the one who still gripped a little too tightly to her inexperience.

He rolled off the bed and leaned down for a quick kiss. "One day that'll be my cock fuckin' your ass." The corner of his lips twitched. "And I'll tell you now, sweetheart, you're gonna love it."

She bit her lip, trying to act unaffected by the wink he gave her before he strode to the bathroom. He was the devil. Only, his touch felt like heaven instead of hell. Scooting under the covers, she glanced at the bedside clock. If she rested her eyes for twenty minutes, she'd still have time to get ready for the bachelorette party.

"Have a quick nap." Mitchell sauntered back into the room and climbed onto the bed to snuggle behind her. "That way you'll have more energy to party tonight."

"More energy to beat you at the honeymoon challenge you mean?"

He hovered over her, placing a kiss on her shoulder. "Yeah, gorgeous. You'll need all the rest you can get with what I have planned."

She ignored the taunt and closed her eyes, resting into the warmth of his chest against her back. "Will you wake me in a little while?"

He brushed his lips against her hair, draping an arm over her waist. "Sure, sweetheart. Just relax and get some sleep."

CHAPTER 2

A LANA AWOKE WITH A START.

"Oh, shit." Mitchell pushed to a seated position, jolting the mattress. "I fell asleep."

"What?" Alana rubbed the lethargy from her eyes and stretched.

He yanked the sheets back and bounced from the bed. "Sweetheart, the guys are already knocking at the door. We slept for over an hour."

She shook her head, her heart changing from the relaxing pace of sleep back into the panicked pulse which had overtaken her for weeks. "No." She glanced at the bedside clock and let out a defeated cry.

Damn it! She jumped from the bed and raced to the bathroom. A five second shower was all she took to clean the evidence of their lovemaking from her body. Then she was out again, running naked into the bedroom to grab her clothes.

"Lookin' good, Al," Mason said from the living room.

She screamed, fumbling over her feet in a hurry to slam the door. *Jerk!*

Why the hell had Mitchell left the room open? She didn't need this angst. Tonight was meant to be relaxing. Well, as relaxing as the challenge to win the choice of her honeymoon destination could be.

Weeks ago, her frustratingly gorgeous fiancé had increased her stress by announcing he wanted to go on a deserted island adventure holiday. The "deserted island" sounded fantastic. The "adventure" part, not so much. The travel website pictured a weather-beaten shack on a white sandy beach, and explained that guests would live the "unique experience of finding food and water on their own."

Not likely.

Every descriptive word the company had boasted made her question Mitchell's sanity. He wasn't the outdoorsy type, and even though he was paying for the majority of the honeymoon, she refused to believe overcoming dehydration and starvation should ever be on any honeymooner's to-do list.

When she'd rallied against the proposal, holding back her claims of his idiocy, he'd smirked, asking her to make a better suggestion. She had. But apparently a luxurious villa in the Maldives wasn't his idea for a perfect honeymoon.

To settle the disagreement, he'd come up with the bachelorette/bachelor party challenge—yet another anxiety filled event she didn't need. Both parties had a list of tasks created by the other group, which needed to be completed within a certain time frame. Whoever finished first would be the victor and get the final say on the honeymoon location.

Snatching her underwear from her suitcase, and the thigh-high, silver shimmer dress from the closet, she yanked them on in record time. Then she raced back to the bathroom to apply make-up at super speed.

"Sorry, I should've closed the door." Mitchell's voice startled her. He came to rest against the doorframe, a white towel fastened around his lean waist. "Babe, you need to relax. Tonight is meant to be fun."

She smiled at his reflection in the mirror and screwed the lid back on her mascara. "I'll be fine once I have a glass of wine or two." Or however many it took to dilute the adrenaline in her veins.

"You look gorgeous, as always."

"Thank you." She dropped the mascara tube onto the counter and strode toward him, placing a quick kiss on his cheek. "I'm going as soon as I get my stockings and boots on."

"OK." He pulled her into his body, and she stabilized herself with a palm to his chest. She fought hard to ignore the heat in his eyes and the seduction on his lips.

No time. No time. No time.

"I'm going to have a shower. I hope you have a great night." He gripped the back of her head and took her mouth in a punishing kiss. When they came up for air, he glanced down at her. "Have fun, just not too much fun, all right?"

Alana tapped on the door of Gabi's Las Vegas suite, already twenty minutes late. She was meeting the girls here to kick off the bachelorette party, while the guys were still in her own suite, consuming bottles of scotch and bourbon.

The clap of high heels echoed from the other side of the heavy wood. There was a beat of silence, then Gabi swung the door wide, two glasses of champagne teetering in one of her hands.

"I was starting to worry," Gabi handed her a glass of bubbling liquid, looking gorgeous in her red stilettos and black party dress.

Alana stepped inside and winced in apology. "Sorry. We fell asleep."

"Oh, I bet you did." Gabi's lips tilted, only the humor didn't reach her eyes.

As the door drifted shut, Alana paused, scrutinizing her friend's features. Something was wrong. She could see it in the slump of Gabi's shoulders and the unconvincing smile. "Everything OK, Gab?"

"Of course." Gabi nodded, taking a sip from her glass and not meeting Alana's gaze.

Alana placed her purse under her elbow and grasped Gabi's forearm as she started down the hall. When her friend stiffened, Alana's already frantic heart thundered in reply. "Gabi?"

Anxious seconds passed before Gabi made eye contact. "I'll be fine." She pasted on a less than enthusiastic smile. "I just need a night out with the girls."

Alana let her hand fall to her side. She'd only seen Blake's fiancée like this once before—at Alana's engagement party. Even through the emotional see-saw of moving her life to the US, Gabi had remained calm and upbeat, barely letting the infectious grin leave her face. "Is everything all right with you and Blake?"

Gabi nodded. "Everything's fine." She pointed a lazy finger down the hall and pivoted on her toes. "The girls are in the dining room waiting for you." Without another word, she strode away.

Alana stood rooted in place, unsure what to do. Moments earlier, back in her own suite, she'd spoken with Blake. He'd been his happy, smart-ass self. Yet Gabi was far from normal. There was no humor in her expression, no light in her eyes.

Taking an unladylike gulp of her champagne, Alana convinced herself to stop worrying. She had enough on her mind without adding more problems to the mix. A night of drinking, games, and laughter would be great for all of them. Well probably not for Alana's mother. Bringing a recovering androphobic woman into the party capital of the world wasn't a great idea. But her mother had been the one to offer her attendance at the bachelorette party. "I'll get to visit Vegas again, and appease my shrink all at once," her mom had said.

Gabi stopped at the end of the short hall, beckoning her forward. "Come on. We started the champagne a while ago. You need to catch up."

Alana allowed herself a relaxed chuckle. Of course they did. The women of her bridal party were more excited about tonight than she was. Kate—her best friend from Richmond, Gabi, and Leah, had giggled like schoolgirls while planning the challenges for the Reckless band members. And they were eager to see what they would receive in return.

"I wouldn't have expected anything less." Alana caught up to Gabi, and they wandered side by side through the archway leading into the dining room.

"Evening, ladies." Alana eyed the large table covered with appetizers and filled champagne flutes. If it weren't for Mitchell's damn challenges, she'd be happy to remain here, with her shoes kicked off, enjoying quiet conversation.

Her mother clucked her tongue. "You're late to your own party."

Having her only parental figure here was going to be a challenge all of its own. Yet Alana was overwhelmed with relief that her mom was pushing boundaries and trying hard to overcome some of the psychological issues that had restricted her to living in relative seclusion for years.

Alana skirted the table, walking past Leah and Kate until she reached her mother, and placed a gentle kiss on her cheek. "You look lovely." The dark pink blouse and jeans were classier than the old, beaten clothes she wore at the retreat, but contrasted from the scanty attire the rest of them wore.

"Thank you. You look..." A scrutinizing gaze travelled up and down Alana's body. "...appropriately dressed for Vegas."

Kate snorted, and Leah cleared her throat.

"*Thanks.*" Alana placed her purse on the table and took another gulp of bubbly liquid.

"Has Mitch emailed the list of challenges yet?" Leah asked, popping a piece of cheese into her mouth.

"Darn!" Alana sat down and opened her purse, retrieving her cell. "I haven't had a chance to forward ours to them." She unlocked her screen and found an unopened email from Mitchell. Before she read it, she scrolled to her draft folder, to where the list for the guys was saved, and pressed send. "Done. OK, let me see what we have to do."

Her stomach fluttered. With the likes of Mason, Sean, Blake, and Ryan, she could imagine the lengths she would need to go to in an effort to win the honeymoon of her choice.

"Umm..." She read the first dare, then had to stop and re-read it again.

"What?" Kate leaned forward in her chair. "Are they bad?"

"No." Alana skimmed the list, her smile growing with every word. "I think we're going to kick their asses, ladies... On the other hand, the guys are going to kill us afterward. The things they've listed are pretty lame in comparison to the stuff we sent."

Gabi took a seat at the head of the table while Kate tapped a manicured nail with impatience. "Well don't just sit there, tell us what they wrote."

"OK, here goes." Alana cleared her throat, trying not to laugh as she re-read the first line. "'Number one—one person has to swallow Alligator Sperm, then have Sex on the Beach with a Cock-sucking Cowboy.'"

"Counts me out," Alana's mom announced. "I know your life has changed due to these *rock stars*. However, there is no way I'm going to participate if it involves sex and alligator sperm."

Leah slapped a hand over her mouth, her cheeks convulsing, her eyes bulging, no doubt trying to refrain from spraying champagne across the table.

"Mom, they're alcoholic beverages. One of us has to consume all three, one after the other, and it's done."

"Oh." Her mother snorted. "Sorry. I heard 'sperm,' and my brain stopped."

"I'll do it," Gabi spoke softly. "God knows I could use a few stiff drinks right now."

Alana gave her a sad smile, and Gabi broke eye contact, peering at the bottom of her champagne flute while she finished downing the contents.

"What's next?" Kate asked.

Alana ignored the tug of conscience that demanded she find out what was wrong with Gabi, and brought her gaze back to her phone screen. "Get something pierced." When she glanced back up, Leah and Kate were frowning.

"Were they specific with the 'something'?" Leah asked in disbelief.

"Nope." Alana shook her head. "Like I said, their dares are pretty lame in comparison to ours. One of us could get our ear pierced, and that would be enough."

"I can't believe they're being so soft." Kate pushed from the table. "I guess it'll give us more time to have fun afterward. We can tick off the challenges within the first hour, then head straight to the Thunder from Down Under." She turned, her heels clicking on the tile as she headed for the kitchen.

Leah nodded. "That sounds good."

"Hold on." Alana held up a hand for them to stop. "Some of these are going to take time, and the rules state we need to have them completed by ten o'clock. Number three says we have to get a five dollar chip from ten different casinos."

"Well at least that's something I can do." Alana's mom offered.

"'Four—Proposition a female stripper and get her phone number.'"

Kate sauntered back into the room and placed another bottle of champagne in the middle of the table. "Put my name down for that one. I'm no stranger to lady action."

Alana's mother made a strangled noise that everyone chose to ignore.

"And 'Number five—Get a Brazilian.'" Alana grinned. "That's an easy one for me, because I already had a booking to get mine done tomorrow."

Leah shook her head in confusion. "Is that all?"

"Yeah." Alana nodded. The guys must have experienced a rare case of chivalry.

"I bet Mason's annoyed as hell," Leah continued. "Mitch had to have vetoed a lot of suggestions."

"I don't care." Alana shrugged and reached for her champagne glass. "As long as I don't have to go on the honeymoon from hell, it doesn't bother me how angry the guys are. But I'd love to see their faces when Mitchell reads out their list."

"**E**ACH OF US HAS TO GET A BEAUTY PROCEDURE DONE AT A SALON," MITCH muttered, not impressed with the first challenge on the list. "And two of those have to include an eyebrow wax and a Brazilian."

"Fuck off," Mason spat. "For starters the whole 'fight for your honeymoon' thing is taking away valuable stripper time. And secondly, you made us pick girlie, lame-ass challenges for the ladies, yet one of us has to get a Brazilian? No fuckin' way."

Mitch heaved a sigh. The last thing he wanted to deal with tonight was Mason's bitching. "Settle down." He took a long chug of his scotch and wondered if tonight's games were such a great plan.

The challenges weren't his idea. He'd only agreed with Leah and Gabi's suggestion to give Alana a night of wild craziness because she deserved it. He knew better than anyone that his fiancée needed to let her hair down. Not only due to the wedding stress, but also because of her secluded upbringing. He wanted her to have the time of her life, he just didn't want to take the blame.

Leah and Gabi planned everything. They even determined the fake honeymoon destination to ensure there was a plausible reason for the challenge. That way, Allie wouldn't be inclined to spend her bachelorette party in her hotel suite, sipping champagne and making placid conversation.

But a male Brazilian? Holy fuck, that's gotta hurt.

The guys stared at him with varying degrees of disbelief and annoyance—Sean, Mason, their two bodyguards, even Ryan wasn't impressed. The one person who didn't seem pissed was Blake, who sat on the couch across from him, legs crossed at the ankles and a knowing grin tilting his lips.

"What are you smiling at?" Sean jutted his chin at Blake. "Did you get laid or somethin'?"

Blake shook his head. "I wish. I spent the last six days in Richmond with grumpy-ass here." He jerked his thumb in Mason's direction. "When I got home, Gabi was surfin' the crimson tide, so I couldn't get lucky if I tried."

"So what's with the smirk?" Ryan asked.

Blake outstretched his arms along the back of the lounge. "Can't a guy be happy to spend quality time with his friends?"

"You know what's on the list, don't you?" Mitch asked, dread growing in his gut. Blake was the only person at the bachelor party who knew the honeymoon issues were fake. Yet there was something more to the gleam in his best friend's eyes.

"Gabi may have given me a hint or two." Blake turned his gaze to Mason. "And why the hell do you have your panties in a bunch about the Brazilian? Didn't we put the same thing on the list for the ladies?"

"There's a big fucking difference, bro," Mason huffed. "Women get their shit waxed all the time."

Sean cleared his throat. "I'll do it."

Stunned silence followed.

Mitch turned his attention to Sean along with everyone else in the room.

"What?" Sean frowned, lowering his gaze to the glass in his hands. "I've had it done before. No big deal."

"You've had it done before," Mason repeated, emphasizing the words with slow deliberation. "You've had the hair ripped from your balls, just for the hell of it?"

"It's not like it's all pain and no gain. I'll get my pole smoked afterward."

"Beauty therapists aren't whores. You know that, right?" Ryan asked. "A

16

blow job isn't part of the deal."

Sean shrugged. "They've never let me down before."

"OK." Blake drawled with widened eyes. "So we've determined who'll get kicked out of the beauty salon first. What else is on the list?"

"'Number two—get a butterfly tattoo in a visible area.'"

More silence.

"I fuckin' hate you for taking my dare of lesbian action off the list," Mason muttered.

"Fine. I'll get the ink," Mitch snapped. "'Number three—Dine and ditch.' I guess we can all participate in that one."

"And when we get arrested, and Leah has to deal with the PR nightmare, it will make this night of hell worthwhile," Ryan offered, rolling his eyes.

Mason leaned over to grab a handful of chips from the packet on the coffee table. "I'm tempted to get caught just to retaliate."

"'Number four—Get ten dollars changed into pennies and have one person carry them around for the remainder of the night.'"

Blake groaned. "That's gonna be a pain in the ass."

Mason scoffed. *That's gonna be a pain in the ass?* "So you protest at carrying change, but you have no problem with hair being ripped from your balls." He quirked a brow. "You've got problems."

"The wax was inevitable," Blake replied. "Get over it."

"'Number five." Mitch lowered his gaze and mumbled over the arguing, hoping to take the sting out of the final challenge. "Do a nude run along the entire length of the Bellagio Fountain."

One of the bodyguards snorted from his leaned position against the wall.

Mitch dropped his cell to the couch cushion beside him and scrubbed a hand down his face. This was a bad idea. A very bad idea which would require a lot of alcohol.

"Well, I think Mitch deserves a round of applause for fuckin' us over." Mason started to clap. "I can't believe you told us to 'go easy on the girls.' We've been royally shafted."

"Oh, come on." Mitch pushed from the couch, needing the extra seconds to figure out how to reply. Mason was right. They'd been bent over and fucked hard, and it was all Mitch's fault. He hadn't expected his sweet and innocent Alana to list challenges that included permanent body markings, illegal activities, and public nudity.

Mitch glanced around the room, wishing his alcohol induced buzz would strengthen so he could get through the night. "Come on guys, don't be such a drag. It'll be fun."

Blake shot him a taunting smile. "Yeah. I wanna hear you repeat that after you get a manly butterfly tattoo."

Mitch clenched his jaw and held in a curse. He was the only one holding this shit together. If he started bitching—and man, he wanted to bitch—the other guys would call it quits. And when the photographic evidence of their completed challenges didn't get sent to the ladies, Alana would stop playing the game.

"Come on." He downed the rest of his scotch and strode to the kitchen, grabbing his wallet and jacket off the counter. "Let's go dine and ditch to get this party started."

They strolled through the Bellagio in a group. Mitch, Mason, and Blake wore baseball caps to shield their faces. The bodyguards strode beside them, dressed in casual jeans and sports jackets to blend in.

Getting spotted in Sin City when one of the crew had to do a nude run later would be a nightmare. Mitch didn't want his ass—or Johnson for that matter—bouncing around the world-wide web. Normally, he wouldn't contemplate a dare that risky. Not even for a substantial sum of money. But the request had come from Alana—his deranged fiancée, and he couldn't let her down. Not when the night's itinerary was concocted for her benefit.

"This place looks good." Sean stopped in front of a burger joint, looking through the windows to the busy room inside. "There's a big enough crowd that we might be able to slip in and out without being caught or recognized."

"Fine," Mason huffed, striding forward to push open the door. "Let's get this shit over with."

Mitch followed, keeping his head low while a waitress seated them at a corner table.

"We'll order straight away," Mitch blurted. There was no point sticking around. They all wanted to get the challenges over and done with.

The woman paused in the process of handing out menus and frowned at him. "OK."

He broke eye contact. The thought of ripping off hard-working people didn't sit well with him. It shouldn't have sat well with Alana either—which made him think she listed the dare in the hopes he would forfeit.

Not a chance.

If he quit, she would too, and he didn't want that.

"We'll get seven cheeseburgers, thanks." Mitch grabbed the front of his cap and yanked it down, not comfortable with the waitress's scrutiny. From the corner of his eye, he watched her take a palm pilot from under her arm and start typing.

"Would you like anything to drink?" she asked.

Mitch started making a mental tally of the money they were going to screw these people for and the guilt churned in his gut. Not even the heavy dose of alcohol he'd consumed in the hotel had calmed his conscience.

"Get us a round of your cheapest beer," Mason answered.

Mitch spared the waitress a glance, noticing how her gaze lingered on the famous front-man's face for longer than necessary.

"Not a problem." She nodded, focusing on each of them one by one, before turning and heading to the kitchen.

"Probably shoulda ordered soda, it'd be cheaper, and the beer will taste like piss," Mason ended on a mutter.

"Finally found a conscience?" Sean taunted. "I didn't think you'd care about ripping people off."

Mason leaned back in his chair, stretched his arms over his head, and perused the room. "I did it for your benefit, not mine. I don't give a shit."

"Yeah, right." Blake chuckled. "I think pretty boy has grown a heart."

Mason snorted. "Not likely."

The beer arrived minutes later, and as Mason anticipated, it tasted like cold piss on the back of Mitch's throat. It wasn't until the food turned up shortly after, that he could chug a few gulps and back it up with a bite of burger.

They ate in silence. Blake continued to smirk, and the bodyguards joined in. At least someone thought the whole set-up was hilarious. Ryan remained quiet, on the border of sulking. Nobody had the balls to ask if his downer stemmed from his problematic marriage. Then there was Sean, who was enjoying every second of Mason's brooding.

Once the food was gone, Mitch took a photo of the empty plates with his phone and sent it to Alana. *Dine and ditch challenge almost complete.* The women would have to take the still image as proof.

As Mitch shoved his cell back into his jacket pocket, Blake nudged his shoulder. "I dare you to down the remaining beer."

Mitch glanced at his glass and the three or so mouthfuls that remained. "No problem."

"No." Blake shook his head and pointed around the table. "I mean the remainder of *all* the beer."

Mitch followed the path of Blake's finger, noting six additional half-full glasses. His head was already at the mellow stage from the scotch he consumed in the hotel suite. Drinking everything on the table would leave him legless.

"No, thanks."

"Come on, you weak prick," Mason taunted. "This is meant to be your bachelor party. Stop being such a pussy."

"Do it. Do it. Do it," Sean started to chant.

"Fine," Mitch snarled, raising his beer to eye the amber liquid with a wince. "Line them up," he ordered, then pressed the glass to his lips. With a deep breath, he tipped the contents into his mouth and chugged before his body could convince him not to.

Gulp after gulp made his stomach revolt, but he continued, determined not to back down. At the very least, Mason should shut the fuck up for five minutes. When he was finished, he handed the empty glass to Sean on his right, while Blake passed him another from his left. They continued the production line for three more drinks until Mitch had to stop and clench his gut.

"Come on, you can do it," Ryan cheered.

Mitch ignored the stares of nearby patrons and eyed the remaining glasses. Then he turned in search of the bathrooms, finding the male door a few yards away. Thankfully, it was within running distance if he needed to puke. With a deep swallow to clear the ass taste from his mouth, he reached out a hand and waited for Blake to place another glass into his palm. And one after the other, he continued to reluctantly drink.

When the final glass was empty, he slammed it down on the table and wiped his mouth with the back of his hand. "Christ, that shit is horrible." He held in a burp, and his stomach roiled with the aftertaste.

"Yup." Sean nodded. "And I can't wait for it to kick in."

Mitch covered his lips with a fist, holding in another burst of air that shot up his throat.

"Well, I'm going to take a leak. I'll catch you guys outside," Blake said, pushing from the table. "I'm not gonna be the last one standing in this challenge."

"What do you want us to do, boss?" One of the bodyguards asked as Blake strode toward the bathrooms.

"Go." He jerked his head in the direction of the doors and frowned when it took a while for his sight to catch up. "We'll meet you at the end of the block." He didn't want them to risk their security licenses if they were caught, and so far nobody had recognized the band, so the threat of a fan stampede was low.

"We'll be fine," Mason reiterated.

The guards nodded and waited for Blake to return from the bathrooms before giving the room a final visual sweep and leaving.

"How are we doing this?" Sean asked, his focus on Mitch. "As soon as you stand up, you're going to hit the floor, so you can't go last."

Mitch shook his head, about to say he'd be fine, then his brain started to swish. "Fuck."

"Yeah, seven half-full glasses of beer mixed with scotch will do that to ya."

"I'll ask for the check," Ryan said with a snigger. "While I'm waiting, you guys can take off and I'll pretend to slip money into the folder before high-tailing it. The waitress is run off her feet at the moment. She's not going to notice us doing a runner."

The four of them eyed each other. Mitch could see the apprehension and guilt on his friends' faces—even Mason—but Mitch's sudden descent into drunkenness made it hard for him to care. "Yeah, sounds good." Anything that involved fresh air and movement to flush the urine-flavored beer from his system would be a healthy choice.

He pushed from his seat, fumbled backward a step, and then righted himself. *Holy shit.* He'd never been a lightweight before. After Alana came into his life, he no longer had to numb his loneliness with alcohol. In fact, he hadn't had more than a few drinks since Christmas—over two months ago.

"Whoa there, tiger." Sean grabbed his shoulder, laughing under his breath. "I think this party might finally be getting started. I say we ditch the challenges and hit the strip clubs."

Mitch shook his head, letting Sean lead him from the restaurant. "No titties until we finish the list." Christ. He had no intention of staring at another woman tonight. Or any other night, for that matter. He just hoped he had the stomach to make it through the tasks before he passed out.

Mason came up beside him, walking close to his side. "You're so whipped it makes me sick."

Mitch halted. Now wasn't the time to visualize someone blowing chunks.

"Come on," Sean tugged at his arm. "Let's get you outside."

Mason moved in front of them, opening the door, and let Mitch shuffle into the cold night air.

"Maybe tonight won't be so bad after all." Mason sniggered and nudged Mitch's shoulder, causing him to stumble.

It took two steps for him to gain his footing, and then he was running straight ahead, barreling into Mason's stomach to wipe the annoying smirk from his face. "You're such a whiny little bitch lately. What's up with you?"

"He lost his muse," Sean said from behind them. "Poor baby is getting whipped by Leah and the label."

Mason pushed Mitch's chest, sending him hurtling into Sean.

"I don't see you helping out with lyrics," Mason snipped. "You nag and complain that you never get any attention, and it's all because you're good for nothing. You literally sit on your ass and hit shit all day."

Sean helped Mitch to his feet and smiled with menace. "I'll be hitting *you* pretty damn soon if you don't quit the attitude."

"Bring it." Mason held up his hands, beckoning him forward.

"Ladies, ladies." Ryan walked up beside them. "I leave you alone for five minutes, and already you're fighting over me." He closed the wallet in his palm and shoved it into his jacket pocket.

"What's with the wallet?" Mitch slurred. "Did you do a runner or not?"

"I had to make it look legit. I played around with my bills for a while, smiled at the waitress, and left. No problems."

"You're looking smug for someone who broke the law," Mason muttered.

Ryan raised his chin and gave a confident nod. "I completed my part for the challenge list. It's up to you guys to do the rest. So yeah, I do feel pretty damn smug."

CHAPTER 4

LEAH SAT DOWN ON THE RECLINED CHAIR IN THE MIDDLE OF THE STERILE BACK room of the tattoo and piercing studio, cool, calm, and totally collected. It was only fitting that she put her hand up for the hardest challenge on their list of tasks. The competition was her idea after all. And so far, the night had been a blast. All she had to do was pierce a part of her body. Easy.

The bottle of champagne she'd consumed back at the hotel had given her the tingling buzz of intoxication. It left her weightless, fancy free, and entirely open to try anything when the gorgeously tanned, muscled and orgasmicly tattooed body artist asked her what she wanted done.

"*My pussy*," had been the first thing to come to mind when his penetrating green eyes met hers. She kept that to herself, though, pressing her lips together so she didn't break into a fit of giggles.

Instead, she'd crossed her legs, clenched her thighs, and listened as he listed the many places able to be pierced. Problem was, she wouldn't mind having his rough hands on every part of her neglected body. Her imagination already anticipated this guy's hot breath grazing her neck, if he focused on her ears. Or the way her skin would shiver if he touched the area around her belly button.

Then his voice grew seductive as he discussed more intimate places.

"How about your nipple? Or the hood of your clit? Or your labia." His bad boy grin widened with every word.

How bout I strip and you can choose the place you like best?

"Excuse me?" he asked, raising a cocky brow.

Holy shit, had she said that out loud? "Umm, what place do you think would be best?"

His eyes glittered, and then his gaze raked her body, down the curve of her breasts, along her waist, to the apex of her thighs. "I always get a buzz from piercing a woman's clit."

Oh, Christ. Her insides melted into a gooey puddle between her legs. It wasn't like her to get swoony over a bad boy. Typically, her lady bits went wild for the sweet guys, the ones who knew how to treat a woman with respect and admiration. The white picket fence and two point five kids stereotype.

She blinked back at him, her drunken side daring her to let him have her clit, while her professional, always in control frame of mind told her to wake the hell up. "Does it hurt?" she asked, biting the inside of her cheek.

He licked his lips, the action causing her to stare at his mouth and the wicked grin that continued to drive her crazy. "It shouldn't, if done properly. There'll be a pinch of pain, and some stinging or warmth until I get the jewelry in. Then things will settle down."

Leah shuffled in the seat, unable to rationalize her thought processes. She wasn't the clit-piercing kind of girl. Not anymore, anyway. Before Reckless and her career choice of Band Manager, she'd been a rock star groupie through and through. Backstage passes, following her favorite musicians on tour, getting in their pants whenever she could. It was a constant adrenaline rush.

Now, she was the level-headed business woman who kept a group of insane rock stars in check. Yet she couldn't ignore the way her core clenched in excitement, or the hardness of her nipples beading against the thin lace of her bra.

"It isn't suitable for everyone, though," he added. "I'd need to check to see if you have enough tissue."

Leah raised a brow. His statement felt like a taunt. Why the hell wouldn't her clit be suitable? She had a pretty kitty, god damn it. "I'm sure mine is fine."

"Oh, I bet it is, sweetheart," he said with a chuckle, and swiveled on his stool to grab a set of disposable gloves from the counter. "If you pull up your dress, and lower your panties, I'll take a look."

She did as instructed, hitching the thigh-high hem over her hips. Lowering her underwear wasn't as easy. She paused, her hands clutching the waistband of her black silk G-string while she closed her eyes.

This wasn't her. Her wild-child days had passed long ago. In fact, the main focus of her life was to navigate the Reckless guys away from doing crazy, drunken crap like this.

Except Ryan.

She'd never had to growl at him. He was her support, the one she depended on to stay level-headed and mature, no matter what situation. Well, he used to be. Now, he didn't speak to her at all.

She opened her eyes, and for a second she didn't see the body artist staring back at her. Instead, she saw the innocent face of Reckless Beat's rhythm guitarist, his light-green irises smiling back at her in friendship—a sight she hadn't seen since their falling out in Australia.

At the time, she'd thought keeping the unfounded gossip about Ryan's wife a secret was the best thing to do. She spent days thinking it over, trying to imagine the situation from their perspective, bringing herself to the point of nausea over the decision she had to make. All that concern and stress for Ryan to then turn around and hate her for the choice she made. He no longer looked at her the same way. He didn't smile, didn't try to make her happy when she had a rough day. The strong relationship she'd had with him had crumpled, and so had her heart.

All because she'd tried to do the right thing. Well, not anymore. To hell with ungrateful musicians and their over exacerbated superiority complexes. She was going to be the reckless one for once. She was going to do something wild and fun, and not stress about making suitable decisions.

She would show the world she could live a little...by getting her clit pierced.

Yeah, it seemed kind of crazy to her, too. Hopefully, in the morning, when the champagne had worn off, it would all make sense.

She raised her chin, grinned at the delicious man before her, and yanked her panties down her thighs. "She's all yours, handsome."

The guy smirked, concentrating on the trimmed patch of curls between her thighs. He raised a Q-tip in one hand. "I need to place this under your hood to check the depth." He did as stated, using one latex covered hand to stretch the skin covering the sensitive bundle of nerves, while his other hand inserted the swab.

She jolted with the touch, breathing heavy and slow to fight her body's need for more. His face was so close to her pussy, his hands all over her heated flesh, and, *oh hell*, the scent of her arousal already permeated the air.

"You doin' OK?" he purred, his focus never leaving her clit.

"Uh...huh." The words came out in sharp pants.

He chuckled, his warm breath brushing her like a caress. "You're sensitive."

"I'd like to think you'd be sensitive, too, if I had my hands all over your shaft."

"If your hands were on my cock, sweetheart, I'd be a hell of a lot more than sensitive."

She cleared her throat and swallowed deep, already anticipating the taste of dark seduction on her lips.

He glanced up at her, disappointment heavy in his eyes. "Unfortunately, company policy states I can't have sex with a client." He continued to stare, his gaze eating her up in the heated silence. "But, if I happen to make you come while I work my magic, then that's a bonus, right?"

She grinned and diverted her gaze. He was so confident. Arrogant. Annoyingly so, just like the guys she worked with, yet she couldn't deny his appeal, or the fact that she hadn't had an orgasm at the hands of someone else in a very long time. "It would be a very nice bonus."

He removed the Q-tip from the hood of her clit and blindly threw it toward the bin in the corner, missing his target. Then his thumb was on her tight bundle of nerves, moving back and forth with slow deliberation.

"Where you from?" he whispered, as two fingers slid between her pussy lips, spreading her open.

She shuddered, holding in a needy moan for penetration. "I..." His touch was teasing, light, yet confident and in control. Warmth grew inside her, the low of her abdomen beginning to ache in the nicest possible way. She wanted him to move faster. Harder. To penetrate her with his skillful touch and make her scream his name...whatever the hell it was. "I...don't know."

What was the question?

He chuckled. "Damn, I wish I could fuck you."

She peered down at him, wishing for the same thing. His gaze was on her slick folds, his teeth biting hard into his lower lip.

She whimpered. Boy, did she want that, too. Her imagination was already in overdrive, picturing what this Adonis had stashed away in his pants. "Are you sure we can't?" she panted, wiggling her hips in desperate need.

He shook his head. "As much as I'd love to have this," his fingers slid inside her pussy, stealing a gasp from her lips as her walls constricted around him, "I love my job more. I can't risk losing it."

Leah focused on the unfamiliar pleasure overtaking her body, and something inside her fractured. She wanted more. Needed it. She could no longer remain content with her all-work-and-no-play lifestyle. She wanted cock. Christ, her body burned for it.

Instead of pleading, she closed her eyes and fought the need to beg. His touch was enough. It would have to be. And in the coming days... weeks...OK, months, she would relive this moment and wonder why the hell she didn't do it more often.

"Doesn't mean I can't make you come," the man whispered. "Getting caught with my dick inside you is one thing. But having my fingers here," he pulsed them in and out, her arousal making the glide of his glove covered digits effortless, "when I need to pierce your pretty little hood, is a lot easier to disguise if someone walks in."

He stretched her, pushing another finger into her channel while his thumb continued to work her clit. "And besides, if I sunk my cock deep inside you, I'd ruin you for all other men."

Leah moaned. His tone showed he was joking, but she didn't doubt him for a minute. This man was made up of wet dreams and involuntary orgasms. He was a heartbreaker, the type to destroy a woman and make her happy about the devastation all at the same time.

She was used to this, though—not being able to enjoy passion due to career choices. Working alongside the five biggest seducers in the music industry, knowing nothing could ever come from their banter, had made her strong. Or stupid. Other women had worked for the management company that employed her, all of them signing the same contract that stated an intimate relationship with a client was a dismissible offense. And she'd seen many of them clear their desks and leave because of it. Yet, Leah felt the same way about her job as the sexy guy with his digits deep inside her. The few seconds of bliss wasn't worth ruining her life.

She opened her eyes and smiled when his green gaze stared back at her.

"You're wreaking havoc on my self-control," tattooed guy muttered.

"Then stop," she taunted, wriggling her ass.

He growled and plunged his fingers deeper, swirling them inside her, brushing her G-spot. "I'm not a quitter."

Oh, she bet he wasn't. What would it be like to be fucked by this man? To be pushed onto his bed and taken hard and fast? With all the cloth hidden tattoos on his body exposed for her exploration.

She ran a hand down her body, picturing the perfection in her mind as she pressed two fingers against the thumb at her clit. The pressure inside her built, the frantic need burning hotter as he took her instruction and worked the tight little bundle of nerves harder.

"As much as I usually encourage women to scream my name when they come, I need you to be quiet, OK, baby?"

She nodded, moving her free hand to cup her breast, tweaking her taut nipple. "I don't know your name."

"Even better," he murmured, and lowered his head to inhale her scent. "Fuck. You smell like heaven. I could bury my face between your thighs and taste you for days."

"Oh, Christ," she gasped. "You're gonna make me come."

"That's the whole point, sweetheart. I want this tight little pussy coming all over my fingers."

Her walls contracted at his words, sending a shot of pleasure to every pulse point on her body. He peered up at her, his lips agonizingly close to her sex, and licked his lips.

Tease! This man was good. Oh, so good in the most frustrating way. He slid his free hand over her exposed abdomen, tickling her responsive skin as he ran his touch under her dress. When he reached her breast, she tensed, the slightest brush against her aching nipples tempting her hovering climax.

"Tell me your name," he asked, continuing to work his fingers in an out of her greedy pussy. "I want to know the name of the woman who is going to haunt my dreams."

It was a line, but a good one nonetheless. It reminded her of the Reckless men, of the arrogance that was too attractive to ignore. "Leah."

"Mmm, Leah." He pinched her nipple, assailing her with a delicious spark of pleasure and pain. "Imagine me calling your name when I'm jerking off in the shower tonight."

The picture of perfection sent her over the edge. She squeezed her eyes shut, and slammed her mouth closed to fight a mewl from escaping. She held tight to her breast, and clutched the side of the chair with her free hand, needing grounding from the bliss trying to sweep her away.

He continued to work her, rubbing with hard pressure against her clit while his fingers kept inside her, swirling around her G-spot. Her pussy clenched, over and over, while her entire body went rigid.

"So fuckin' hot," bad boy muttered.

Leah jolted with the last spasms of climax, still picturing the wet and aroused man in her mind, as her high faded. Then his touch was gone, his fingers gliding from her tight heat, his palm no longer cupping her breast.

She opened her eyes and found him staring down at her with an intensity that held her captive. He didn't speak, didn't move, just continued to watch her with ferocity as she panted to catch her breath.

"I shouldn't have denied myself," he whispered, yanking off his gloves. "I'm going to regret not fucking you for the rest of my life."

Leah chuckled, and a smile tilted his lips. She needed the ego boost. Being surrounded by men with superiority complexes had played havoc on her confidence, yet this man had given it all back to her, and then some. "Thank you."

"No need to thank me, sweetheart." He turned on his stool and threw his gloves into the bin in the corner. "Watching you come undone was thanks enough."

Heat crept into her cheeks. *No. No. No. Don't sober up now.* She shook off the embarrassment and as he pushed along the floor on his stool and retrieved a clean pair of gloves from the counter. He worked at the bench to the side of the room, opening packets, removing instruments from what she assumed was the sterilization unit, and placed them on a covered steel tray.

"But now that all the fun is over, it's time for me to leave my mark on that tempting hood of yours." He slid back across the floor with the tray in his hands and placed it in the holder to the left of her chair. "Would you prefer a vertical or horizontal piercing?"

He talked, non-stop, entirely in his element about things she couldn't fathom, while he removed her G-string. Jewelry options, pain and healing timeframes, precautions and the risk of infection. None of it sunk in. All she could do was nod and agree with what he thought was best. Next thing she knew, he was positioned between her thighs again, inserting a tiny silver rod under her hood. She closed her eyes and prayed to wake up from her freakishly out of character dream. Why the hell was she prettying up a place that nobody else would ever see? She opened her mouth, trying to build the courage to pull out of her decision when he cut her off.

"Take a deep breath in."

She did as instructed and squealed when the fires of hell erupted in her most treasured body part. "Holy shit." It wasn't a scream. Not really. More like a high-pitched call.

Cold pressure doused the pain, and she breathed deep to calm herself. "It's a saline swab," bad boy announced. "It's easy sailing from here, sweetheart. I'll put the jewelry in, which may feel a little uncomfortable, and after that there should be little to no pain."

Leah opened her eyes and nodded. She watched as he bedazzled her rudder, thankful for the alcoholic buzz numbing her senses.

"OK, we're all done." He yanked off his gloves with a snap and eyed his handiwork. "You'll be happy with the results. It's like a homing device for pleasure. Guys won't have to search for that elusive clit anymore."

"Now all I need is a man," she drawled, drawing her thighs together with caution.

Bad boy stopped her, placing a hand on her knees. "Tell you what, if you don't have a guy worshiping you by this time next year, come find me. I'll show you a weekend you'll never forget."

Leah wanted to laugh, but the happiness wouldn't flow from her lips. This man was gorgeous, confident, and sweet in a rough and dominant kind of way, yet the thought of a weekend alone with him made her sad. Her days of being wild and free were over. She wanted a husband to love her, not a stranger to share a few days of heated passion. And this man wasn't her type. She wished he was. Or maybe this was fate's way of telling her she needed to stop thinking about men she couldn't have.

"I'll take your silence as a brush off."

"No!" Leah sat up straight, not wanting to offend the man who'd unselfishly pleasured her. "I was daydreaming."

He handed over her G-string, his expression devoid of humor. "Well, whoever you were thinking about needs a kick in the ass for not staking a claim on you."

"I wasn't thinking of anyone in particular." She wasn't. There wasn't a man on her radar at the moment. Nobody suitable to give her heart to, anyway.

"Sure you weren't," he taunted, seeing right through her. His stare was uncomfortable, like he knew the thoughts she was trying to hide even from herself. "You're a gorgeous woman, Leah. If he doesn't want you, then find a better man who does."

Ten minutes later, Leah shuffled from the back room into the reception area, her confidence now replaced with chagrin. Bad boy followed behind her. His taunting grin still consumed her mind, along with the chuckle he'd released when she squealed from the needle's penetration.

"What the hell did you get done?" Gabi asked, striding toward her.

Leah winced and pulled the strap of her handbag higher on her shoulder. If she ignored the question, it might go away. She'd sobered up and had more than a few moments of clarity to acknowledge her stupidity. Receiving sexual pleasure from a stranger was a dumb idea. The piercing was even dumber. Yet, the thing that nagged her the most were a few simple words—*whoever you were thinking about needs a kick in the ass*. Was she that transparent?

"Leah?" Gabi spoke again.

Leah let out a sob. She didn't want to voice her stupidity. She was meant to be smart, god damn it. With a deep breath she spoke, "It took a sudden, excruciating burst of pain—*that felt nothing like a pinch*—to sober me up and realize what a dumb idea this was."

Alana came to stand beside Gabi, her lips pressed together in contained laughter. "You look pale."

"Show us the piercing," Kate said, stepping forward. "We need a picture to send to the guys."

Oh, hell no!

Leah shook her head, and sexy bad boy broke into laughter from behind her. "I can't do that."

"Why?" Gabi asked. "What did you get done?"

Leah glanced from one lady to the next. Alana, Gabi, and Kate held varying expressions of humor, while Mrs. Shelton frowned in concern.

"I got my…" She cleared her throat and gestured to her crotch.

Alana's mom gasped.

Gabi burst into laughter, the first free-spirited reaction Leah had witnessed from Blake's fiancée all night. "You did your clit?" she asked.

Leah continued to wince as she nodded. "Why would I do something so stupid? I don't understand. I walked in there contemplating an earring, then sat down and became distracted."

Kate eyed the tattooed stud behind the counter and grinned. "I don't blame you."

"Yeah, me either," Alana muttered, "But you'll still have to prove it to the guys."

Leah's stomach nose-dived. "No way." She shook her head with vehemence. "They'll have to take my word for it."

"Has Mason ever acted like a guy who would take your word for it?" Alana sniggered.

A whimper escaped her lips. There was no way any of those guys were seeing her private parts. They would never let her live it down, not to mention she could lose her job. Maybe she should go back in and get her ears done.

Gabi winced then covered it up with a cheesy smile. "It's OK, we'll work it out."

Leah sighed, turning to pay the sexy man behind the counter. She concentrated on tidying her purse, unable to look him in the eye, until he handed back her credit card and didn't let it go. He held it tight between his fingers until her gaze met his.

"Remember what I said, Leah," he spoke in a soft tone. "Come find me if you need help convincing yourself how gorgeous you are."

She ignored the fluttering of her heart, and smiled. "Thank you. As much as I'd like to...finish what we started, I hope you never see me again."

"Yeah, sweetheart. It's a double-edged sword for me too."

He released her card, and she gave him one final seductive grin before turning her back and walking over to the circle of waiting ladies. "Let's get out of here. I need a stiff drink."

"No problem." Alana placed an arm around Leah's shoulders. "Next stop is a strip club."

CHAPTER 5

GABI DIVERTED HER GAZE FROM THE BARED BREASTS OF THE SLIM WOMAN ON stage and stared at the glasses lining the strip club table in front of her—a shot of Alligator Sperm, a tall glass of Sex on the Beach, and another shot of Cock-sucking Cowboy. This wouldn't end pretty. She'd already tried to drown her sorrows in champagne, and the alcohol had gone straight to her head, now throbbing with the loud stage music.

The sweet bubbly liquid hadn't helped her mood, but the three more drinks may numb her senses enough to forget her pain. She wanted to enjoy herself, for Alana's sake, yet all she could find were tiny bursts of happiness that flittered away with the next breath. Like when Leah had announced her clit hood piercing. *That* had been funny, yet Gabi's humor died within seconds, replaced with the suffering she'd been going through for days.

"What are you waiting for?" Leah asked. "Get your drink on."

Gabi sighed, and pasted on a smile, hoping to fake her enjoyment. "You know I'm going to be pissed as a cricket after this, don't you?"

Alana frowned. "I thought you wanted to do this. If it's going to annoy you, don't do it."

Gabi rolled her eyes. One day, hopefully in the near future, she would no longer have to explain Australian slang to her friends. "No, I mean 'pissed' as in drunk, not angry."

"There's a difference?" Kate asked over the thump of heavy bass.

"There is in Australia."

"Just do it fast. One. Two. Three. Then you're done." Alana held up her phone, videotaping Gabi's dare so they had proof to send to the guys.

"OK, here goes." She took a deep breath, ignoring the sadness that clawed at her chest and downed the first shot in a quick swallow. *Bang*. She slammed it back down on the table. "Damn, that was nice." Sweet, creamy with a slight tangy aftertaste.

"Don't stop," Kate screeched. "You need to do them straight after each other."

Gabi lowered her gaze to the remaining drinks so she didn't glare at Alana's best friend. "Cheers." She raised the glass of Sex on the Beach, then placed it to her lips and sculled. Her throat glugged as her stomach became heavy. Not a good sign when the sole item lining her gut was alcohol.

Bang. She slammed the second glass down and gasped for air. Before she contemplated backing out, she stared at the tiny camera lens on Alana's phone and downed the remaining shot.

Bang.

All done.

Her insides swirled, revolting at the liquid poison. "I think I'm gonna be sick." She placed a hand on her belly and time stopped. Her instinct to touch her stomach was normal, yet it made her wince, and she squeezed her eyes shut to stem the tingling in her eyes.

"Toughen up, princess." Leah spoke beside her. "At least you didn't have to get a piercing."

Gabi opened her eyes, already thankful that the alcohol was heating her blood, lessening her emptiness. She glanced at Leah and smiled. "Why you didn't pick your ear or even your tongue to pierce is beyond me. But have fun proving it to the guys."

"Guys, shmys," Leah slurred, taking a large gulp of her fruity drink.

"I wouldn't have a problem proving it," Kate cackled. "If the others are half as talented between the sheets as Blake, I'd show them all."

Umm. What the fuck now? Gabi frowned, while dread added to the mix

36

of churning emotions coursing through her body. "Excuse me?" She didn't withhold her glare this time. "What the hell did you say?"

Kate's eyes widened. "Um."

"Um?" Gabi raised a brow. "Please tell me you haven't slept with my fiancé." She was so sick of this. Sick of women fawning over him, chasing him, trying to seduce a man who was clearly off the market.

"Um…" Kate shot a panicked glance at Alana, then turned back to Gabi. "Yeah, I got that part."

"It was before he met you," Alana interrupted. "Back when Mitchell and I first hooked-up."

"Jesus Christ," Gabi snapped, her hands beginning to tremble. Her sanity began to break, her head pounding harder with each pained breath. "Has anyone here *not* slept with Blake?"

Mrs. Shelton slowly raised her hand.

"Well thank fuck for that," Gabi muttered.

Alana shook her head. "You know I haven't slept with him."

Gabi turned to the bride-to-be and narrowed her gaze. Alana had seen Blake naked, had watched him jerk himself to completion, and given him the viewing pleasure of her having sex with Mitch—same damn thing. Yet she couldn't blame her friend. It was in the past, and Alana knew better than to bring up conversations that would create hostility between them.

"What about you, Leah?" Gabi shifted her focus, trying hard not to let her tempestuous mood take hold, and failed miserably. "Have you slept with him? Or seen him naked? Or let him watch you have sex?"

"Girlfriend, I'm so damn drunk right now, I can't tell if you're grumpy or just messin' with us. I will admit to seeing him naked, though. That guy has the finest ass this world has ever seen." Leah's eyes gleamed in enthusiasm as she nodded her head in jerky movements. "Yumm-ohh."

Bloody hell. She didn't need this. Her mind was already filled with enough insecurities without going back to worrying about Blake's man-whoring days. It didn't matter that he'd done all the dirty deeds before they met in person. His past still had the ability to eat away at her when she was low. Women continued to flirt with him—at the grocery store, at restaurants, in the elevator of their apartment building when Gabi was standing right beside him. And even though he always ignored it, or brushed it off with polite indifference, it continued to make her feel like the lesser party in their relationship.

"I'm sad to admit, I haven't seen his front-junk," Leah continued, not picking up on Gabi's torment. "Although, from Alana's description and Kate's enthusiasm, I guess you're one very lucky lady, Gabrielle Smith."

Gabi ignored the comment and grabbed her purse from the table. "I need some fresh air." She didn't want to ruin Alana's night, but if she remained here, surrounded by women who had shared intimate moments with her fiancé, she would lose the single thread she held to her sanity.

It had been two days since her life had been torn apart. Two days filled with crying in isolation, suffering from mental anguish unlike anything she'd ever experienced. Yet, she'd vowed to hold herself together until the end of Alana's wedding. Only two more days to get through, and then she could crumple.

"Don't go." Leah made a drunken attempt to clutch Gabi's arm and missed. "I was joking about Blake's body." She peered up at Gabi with pleading eyes. "Well, OK, maybe I wasn't. You're lucky to have such a hottie. He's every woman's wet dream."

"Including yours?" Gabi asked.

Leah jerked back in shock. "Hell, no."

Gabi bit her tongue, wishing she could sober up to stop the hateful thoughts swimming around in her head. As much as the conversation hurt, she knew Leah and Alana would never talk like this if they knew what she was going through.

"Where are you going?" Alana's mom asked with parental concern.

"Just outside the front doors. I won't be long."

Leah opened her mouth to protest, but Alana cut her off. "Let her go. I'm not really fond of sticking around a female strip club anyway. Once Kate chats up a stripper and gets her number we'll follow you."

Gabi glanced away from the sympathy in Alana's eyes and took her first step toward the entrance of the club. The floor swayed, followed by her head, and then her stomach voiced its reluctance to hold the liquid it contained. Quickly, she diverted her course to the female restrooms where she heaved every last ounce of alcohol, along with her dignity. Once the private humiliation was over, she freshened up in the basin. She didn't bother looking at herself in the mirror. Her haunted gaze would only compound the situation. Instead, she stumbled on numb legs to the cloak room, retrieved her coat, and made her way outside.

She closed her eyes when the cold air hit her skin, and raised her face to the sky. The comfort of darkness helped, a little. Yet she still yearned for the peace of the Australian starlit skies and fresh Queensland air. Not the manic, tainted surroundings of Vegas, with the night lit up as if it were day.

People strode around her, carrying on with life even though hers had stopped spinning. She didn't know what to do. Didn't know how to move forward. Or how to dislodge the torment and confusion.

On any other day—before the drama of this week had shattered her—she would've loved experiencing the debauchery of her first trip here. Right now, though, she wanted to be alone. She hadn't even had time to talk to Blake. He'd come home from Richmond with minutes to spare before leaving for Vegas, and her news wasn't something she could spring on him in public.

"Gabi?" Alana's voice called soft and low, barely registering over the excitement of the city.

She opened her eyes, glancing at Alana's worried expression before lowering her gaze.

Alana's hands brushed Gabi's coat covered shoulders. "Tell me what's wrong."

Gabi sucked in a breath, wavering, so close to crumpling. Her body began to shiver, from the cold or belated shock, she wasn't sure.

Alana's arms enveloped her, holding her in a tight hug. "Do you want me to call Blake?"

Gabi shook her head and squeezed her eyes closed, releasing a trail of scorching tears down her cheeks. "I'm going to go back to the hotel." She spoke into Alana's shoulder. The Bellagio was only a five-minute walk from here. "I don't want to ruin your night any more than I already have."

"I'm not leaving you alone, Gabi." Alana held her tighter. "Why don't I take you back to your suite, and we can watch a pay-per-view."

Gabi continued to shake her head and pulled out of her friend's arms. She stepped back, putting distance between them, letting the frigid air cool her heated face.

"Then tell me what's wrong," Alana continued. "I may not be able to help, but talking might make it better."

Gabi sucked in a ragged breath until her lungs filled to capacity. She couldn't say the words, otherwise Blake would've known by now. And once she was strong enough to speak, he would be the first to know.

Gabi swiped at the tears lining her cheeks and laughed, hoping to placate Alana. "I'm fine. Just having a drunken breakdown. Give me five minutes to pull myself together, and I'll come back inside."

The last thing she wanted to do was walk back into the strip club, but if she didn't get the alone time necessary to regain her resolve, she didn't think she'd be able to get through the rest of the night, let alone the entire weekend. "I promise," she continued. "Once I settle down, I'll find you."

It wasn't a lie. Gabi did want to enjoy Alana's bachelorette party. She just wasn't sure if settling down was an option she had any control over.

CHAPTER 6

SEAN CLIMBED FROM THE CAB AND FOLLOWED THE GUYS INTO THE BEAUTY salon. He had to admit, the night wasn't as lame as he expected. When he'd been told their plan of strippers and booze was being changed to a pansy-ass game of challenges, he'd been annoyed. But Mason's bitchy attitude made the lack of naked women worthwhile.

Not that he liked seeing his friends struggle...well, yeah, that may be a lie. When it came to Mason, Sean was happy to watch the guy suffer. The band front-man had the monopoly on cocky arrogance, so being a witness to his stress over the upcoming album had turned into a pleasurable experience. The rest of the band knew he'd kick out of the funk soon enough. None of them were worried. Instead, they enjoyed the fuck out of Mason's loss in confidence.

Up ahead, Mitch held the door to the salon open, and Sean stepped inside. The acrid scent of nail polish and incense hit him like a physical blow. He ignored it, sinking into the zone. He had a date with hot wax and a sexy beautician. What more could a guy ask for?

"The bachelor party?" a middle-aged woman asked from behind a waist-high counter. She had dark wavy hair and a friendly smile that reached her light hazel eyes. Sean studied every inch of her, imagining her hands roaming his crotch, the way the warm wax would tingle against his skin, the sharp sting of pain and pleasure that would follow.

"Yeah," Mitch murmured from beside him, his shoulders swaying as he pulled the door closed.

"Great." The woman clapped her palms together. "I have a room set up for the waxing, but I was told there would be three more treatments specified once you arrive. What else would you like done?" She handed a brochure to Ryan.

Mason snatched the paper and began scanning the list.

"I'm easy," Blake spoke from the back of the group. "I'll get my nails painted a pretty shade of black."

"Bullshit," Mason spat. "If I'm getting my eyebrows waxed, you have to get something better than that."

"Nah." Blake gave a lazy shake of his head. "I really don't."

A grin spread across Sean's face. This truly was an awesome night.

"Lighten up, asshole. This is meant to be fun." Mitch stumbled forward, grabbed the brochure from Mason and handed it back to the woman with an apologetic smile. "Why don't you surprise us? Just be kind, OK?"

The woman inclined her head. "Sure. Let's get started." She outstretched her arm, gesturing toward the hall. Her hands were small and delicate—not big enough to wrap around Sean's cock, yet he could already anticipate the smoothness of her palms against his shaft. "Whoever is getting the Brazilian can go to the first room on the left. Maree is waiting for you."

Maree? Damn, he'd become used to the thought of fucking this lady's pretty little mouth. No biggie. Nine out of ten beauticians were hot. It was one of the main reasons he kept coming back for more.

"And you," she glanced at Blake, "can take a seat at the nail counter over there." She pointed to a table with an overhead lamp in the far corner of the room. "I'll be able to paint your nails for you."

Sean turned to the guys, a grin plastered on his face, and gave them a salute. "I'll see you in a little while."

Mitch chuckled, his intoxication showing in the glaze of his eyes. "Have fun, you crazy bastard."

Oh, he would. No doubt about it. He strode down the hall, stopping at the first door and slid it across, stepping into the dimly lit room. Candles burned in the corners of the counter stretching along the far wall, and a massage table sat in the middle of the room, draped with a small white towel and one of those paper thongs he'd grown to hate.

A curvy woman stood with her back to him, her light strawberry-blonde hair pulled into a ponytail and resting against her spine. Her concentration sat on the container in front of her, her gloved hands stirring a stick through what he knew would be warming wax. She glanced over her shoulder, her gorgeously smooth hair swishing around her neck to land against her chest. The room was dark, seductively so, yet he still noticed the blue in her irises and the spark of recognition in her gaze.

"Hi." He grinned at her, his cock already thickening, eager for action. "I'm Sean Taiden."

Her mouth opened, then snapped closed. Shyness crept into her ocean eyes, and she smiled up at him under delicate lashes. "I know who you are."

Really? He quirked a brow. It wasn't often that people did. Yeah, Reckless Beat were famous—Mason, Mitch, and now even Blake being household names. But Sean was the faceless guy who sat at the back of the stage. As Mason would say, he literally sat on his ass and hit shit all day. Nobody knew him. Although she did look familiar. "Have we met before?"

She shrugged and turned around to concentrate on stirring the wax. "I'm from Richmond."

Ahh, a woman from his home town. "So we know each other?"

"No. And don't worry, you wouldn't remember me." She placed the stick on the counter and turned back to face him. "Have you had a Brazilian before?"

"Yeah." And the more he thought about getting another, the harder his dick became. He pulled his shirt over his head. Entirely unnecessary seeing as though she only needed to focus on his crotch, he just wanted to see her eyes brighten with his show of skin.

She didn't disappoint.

He couldn't afford not to have a flawless body when it came to pussy. If it wasn't for his physique, every groupie would pass him over for Mason. He fucking hated getting scraps.

He reached for his belt and unfastened the clasp.

She stared at him with wide eyes, her mouth agape. "OK. Well, I'll leave you to put on the paper underwear, for modesty's sake." She didn't move, simply stood there, watching as he toed off his shoes and undid the first button of his jeans.

"I'm not modest," he drawled, and pushed his pants and boxers down his thighs.

She gaped for long seconds, and then swiftly turned back to the counter. "I guess not," she whispered and cleared her throat. "If you'd like to lie down on the table we can get started."

He did as requested, lying across the thin layer of paper draped down the length of the cushioned table. He rested his hands behind his head and stared at Maree as she turned with a stick full of wax.

She didn't make eye contact. Her face now devoid of emotion as darkness crept into the top of her cheeks. "Can you turn one of your legs out and hold your...penis to the side, please?"

He chuckled, enjoying her discomfort. "Sure."

She leaned over his package and used her fingers to make the already tight skin of his sac, taut. With efficient strokes, she made two trails of wax, one along the lower side of his shaft, and the other over his balls. Then she turned, placing the application stick into a bin, and came back to blow on the cooling wax, lightly tapping it to see if it was set.

"Ready?" she asked.

He didn't reply, merely grinned down at her until her blush grew darker.

The first rip of the wax stung. The usual burst of pain filled his lungs and made his cock pulse. Normally, he wasn't a masochist. Pain in the bedroom didn't crank his chain. Yet once he had a stranger's hands on his balls and the thrill of customers waiting in the reception area, things changed.

Maree continued to apply the wax and remove it minutes later. Apply and remove. Apply and remove. Until his cock was so sensitive, the mere grip of his own hand made him want to come. She didn't speak. Refused to make eye contact, yet her sassy little tongue kept coming out to moisten her pretty pink bottom lip.

"Done," she announced, snapping off her plastic gloves and placing them in the bin.

"Really?" he drawled. "You're really finished with me?"

She glanced at him in confusion, and he released his erect cock, letting it bob against his stomach. Her eyes widened, the shyness creeping back into those big blue irises.

"There's nothing else you want to do?"

Her gaze moved to his shaft and then back to his face. "I shouldn't." She paused to swallow. "I'd get in a lot of trouble."

"You won't." He reached for her hand and pulled her close, placing a kiss on her knuckles. "I can be quiet, if you can."

She bit her lip, and ever so slightly, her mouth tilted in a shy smile, exposing tiny dimples.

He took the passion in her gaze as a sign of approval, and sat up, maneuvering his legs to hang over the side of the table. He dragged her forward, securing her between his thighs and lifted her chin with his fingers. She stared at him, a mix of awe and surprise in her features.

"I want to kiss you," he murmured, leaning in so their faces were mere inches apart.

She replied with a whimper and closed her eyes, her hands coming to rest at his sides. He chuckled against her lips, loving her sweet acquiescence, and swept his mouth against hers. She moaned into the kiss, her fingers hesitantly moving over the smooth skin where his legs joined his waist.

"Touch me." He spoke into her mouth. "Grab my cock."

Slowly, she complied, drawing her palms over his skin until her nails brushed the length of his shaft. He tensed, so fucking close to exploding, and deepened the kiss. He devoured her, breathed in her needy whimpers, tasting the sweetness on her tongue.

"We need a condom," he whispered.

She nodded and stepped back, allowing him to push from the table and stride the few steps to retrieve his jeans from the floor. He scrounged through the pockets, grabbing one of the three condoms he'd placed there—because a guy never knew how lucky he'd get—and maneuvered back around to her side.

He stopped when they were toe to toe and grasped her hips, lifting her to sit on the table. Without preamble, he gripped the waistband of her navy pants and began to pull, dragging them down her thighs, over her knees.

He yanked them off, along with her black shoes, then stepped back to admire her soaked white panties. The virginal, lace underwear spoke of inexperience, yet the slight gleam in her eye showed a hidden seductress waiting to break free.

"Spread 'em." He nudged his knee against hers and pushed between her legs.

Damn the nail polish permeating the air. If they were back in his hotel suite, he'd be able to smell her arousal, be able to taste her sweetness on his tongue.

"Open this for me." He handed her the condom packet and grinned at the seconds it took her to blink back to reality. "You OK?"

She nodded.

"Good." He grabbed the waistband of her panties and yanked them off, making her gasp with his roughness. Once the thin material hit the floor, he stared at the apex of her thighs, enjoying the tempting sight of her hairless pussy. "Nice."

"Glad you approve," she replied, spreading her legs a little wider.

He loved the female body. He could stare for hours, play for days, he would never get enough. Reaching out his hand, he waited for the condom. With shaky fingers, she placed it in his palm, and three seconds later, he was suited and ready for action. He gripped her ass, pulling her forward to hover on the edge of the table. She gasped, clinging to his shoulders and hissed out a breath when his cock found the entrance of her sex.

"Get ready, sugar." He slid the head of his shaft between her folds, gauging her arousal, testing her need. He teased her until she began to whimper, her gentle fingers now gripping the back of his neck tightly. "You're not a screamer are you?"

She shook her head. "No," she panted.

"OK, then." In one thrust, he sank home, enveloping his shaft in tightness, causing him to stifle a groan of utter satisfaction. Her nails dug into his skin, and she lowered her head to rest against his shoulder.

"Do me hard," she begged.

He growled, loving her style, enjoying her loss of inhibitions. He plunged into her, the harsh slaps of skin against skin echoing in the room. She was slick, his cock driving in an out of her, smooth as silk.

"What's your trigger?" he asked, wanting to bring her along with him as he approached the finish line. He'd had enough women to figure out they were all different. Some liked nipple play, others clit stimulation, or anal. He enjoyed everything. Most of all, he appreciated the way they succumbed to pleasure.

She stiffened and pulled back to look him in the eye. "I don't understand." Innocence crept into her features, and he didn't want it there. He wanted her undone, writhing against him, her covered breasts thrusting for friction.

And why the hell hadn't he taken her top off? Shit, he was a man on a mission tonight. Normally, he was all over those puppies.

"What do you like? How do I make you feel good?"

Her dimples came out again, and she broke eye contact. "Just do me harder." She leaned back to rest one hand against the massage table behind her, while the other slid down her waist to her clit.

Christ. She may be shy talking about sex, but she didn't have a problem helping herself reach climax. He watched, fascinated as she worked the tips of her manicured fingertips over her clit. It was so cute. So feminine. Enough to make his balls tighten at the beauty. He gripped her hips, pounding hard enough that his sac slapped against her ass. She sucked in a breath and winced. For a moment, he thought he'd hurt her, but she narrowed her eyes, her greedy stare daring him to continue. Her nails dug into the table, and with the following thrusts the wooden legs moved, jumping against the floor with sharp, squeaking protests.

Maree closed her eyes and began to whimper with each penetration, her hand frantically gliding back and forth over her nub. Her whimpers became faster, louder, and he hoped like fuck she was about to come because he was already there.

He arched his back, slamming home over and over until his orgasm exploded. "*Fuck,*" he growled through clenched teeth and squeezed his eyes shut, enjoying the pleasured jolts that overtook him. She clung to him, her pussy milking him as it contracted with her own climax.

As the final waves of pleasure left his body, she lowered her legs from his waist. They breathed into one another, no emotion, no cloying commitment, just the awesomeness of gratification tilting their lips.

"That was fucking brilliant," he panted, cupping the back of her head to leave a slapping kiss on her lips. She whimpered with a nod, boosting his ego with her dazed expression. She was lost, still hovering in the space between climax and reality.

He grinned and stepped back. He disposed of the condom and strode around the table to get his clothes. Another Brazilian job well done. Man, he loved this shit.

"I can't believe that just happened." She glanced over her shoulder before pushing from the table and righting her shirt. "I gather it's not a first for you."

He pulled on his pants, unable to keep the smirk from his face. "No. Not a first. I like sex after a woman has her hands all over my sac."

Her lips lifted at one side, and she lowered her head, turning back into the shy woman he'd met when he first barged in. The more he glanced at her, the more the image of her face haunted him. He knew her, or knew *of* her. He just couldn't figure it out.

"What school did you go to?" He yanked his shirt over his head and waited for a reply.

"Godwin High," she murmured.

Jackpot. "That's where I must've seen you before." But she was younger, three or four years at least.

She nodded and turned back to the counter to wash her hands. "Yeah."

Cool. Problem solved. He shrugged. "Well, I'll go get Mason so you can do him too."

She shot him a petrified look over her shoulder, her eyes wide.

"Shit." He laughed, long and loud, letting the noise reverberate off the walls. "I didn't mean *do* him. I meant the waxing. I'll send him in so you can start his eyebrows."

"Oh." Her posture relaxed and she shook her head. "Glad you clarified. I'm not sure this body could withstand two rock stars in one night."

Sean let his gaze glide over her curves and back up to those sparkling blue eyes. "Honey, I'm damn sure it could."

CHAPTER 7

MITCH SAT IN THE RECEPTION AREA, FLICKING THROUGH A NAMELESS magazine. This shit just got worse. Now he had to go through the rest of the night with a face full of bridal make-up. He'd been smothered in lipstick, eye shadow, blush, along with powder and cream crap they smeared over his face, and fucking fake eyelashes. He resembled a fifty cent hooker who hadn't scored a job in years.

And the solitary reason he'd sat through the treatment was because he was too drunk to get up. The twenty-minute reprieve from reality had brought him time to drink a few glasses of water—as long as he didn't smear his lipstick—and stop the room from spinning.

Now it merely tilted.

Blake already had his nails painted black. Ryan put his hand up for a fake tan, Sean was getting unthinkable shit done to his balls, and Mason was up next. Mitch looked forward to seeing how the arrogant little cocksucker withstood the sting of wax, and the sooner the better. He couldn't sit through another five minutes of the singers sniggering from the other side of the room.

"You're next, pretty boy," Blake said from beside Mitch, jutting his chin in Mason's direction.

The three of them turned to focus on Sean striding back into the room.

"Did it go as planned?" Blake asked.

Sean shrugged, a smirk spreading across his lips.

"Bullshit," Mason spat. "I don't believe you."

Sean chuckled. "I was happy with the service. As always." His focus passed Mitch before doing a double take. "What the fuck is up with your face?"

Mitch groaned. *Please, please, please, let me get through the night without photographic evidence.*

"He got shafted with the bridal make-up experience," Mason taunted. "Ain't he pretty?"

Mitch glared, wishing for death ray vision to turn the fucker to ash. "Yeah, she asked me who I wanted to look like, and I told her yo' momma."

"Well, they didn't do a very good job," Blake added. "His mom has more facial hair."

"Don't start this shit now," Sean laughed. "I wanna get outta here. Mace, hurry up." He jerked his head in the direction of the hall. "I'll come with you for moral support."

"Me too." Mitch pushed from his chair. "I've gotta see this." He followed down the hall, Blake at his back. Mason strode ahead, entering the room, but Sean blocked the entry before the rest of them could follow.

"Can I see the challenge list again?" Sean asked, holding out his hand for Mitch's phone.

"Sure." Mitch pulled the cell from his jacket pocket and scrolled to the email from Alana. "What do you want it for?"

Sean's lips tilted in a smirk. "Clarification." He grabbed the phone and focused on the screen for a few silent seconds. His lips widened, and he leaned in close. "You know the list states 'get *an eyebrow* wax', not 'eyebrows'," he whispered. "What if the girls meant one eyebrow completely waxed off?"

Mitch snorted, picturing Mr. Pretty Boy sulking around Sin City with a lopsided face.

"What are you assholes laughing about?" Mason called from inside the room.

"Nothin'. You just lie down and let the lady do her job," Sean answered, then leaned into Mitch. "You don't want to lose the challenge on a technicality, do you?"

"You're serious?"

"Deadly. He's been a dickhead all night. Why not give him a proper excuse to be a bitch?"

Mitch's drunken side loved the idea. There was no way the beautician would agree, though. She may be young. It didn't mean she was stupid… then again, if she slept with Sean…

"Maree, can I speak to you for a second?" Sean called over his shoulder.

"Oh, shit," Blake muttered. "I'm going inside. I haven't had enough alcohol to be a party to this."

Blake disappeared into the darkened room, and Mitch knew he should follow—for self-preservation's sake, at the very least. But Sean was right, Mason deserved it. The alcohol flooding Mitch's system chanted that the pretty boy needed a full dose of his own medicine. Didn't mean he wanted to be one of the instigators, though.

"I'll meet you inside," Mitch said, smiling at the young strawberry-blonde who shuffled into the hall.

Sean sniggered. "Chicken."

"Yep."

Mason lay on the massage table in the center of the room, his gaze following Mitch as he wandered in to lean against the wall next to Blake.

"What are you guys planning?"

Blake put his palms up in surrender. "I'm not planning shit, bro."

Mason's gaze narrowed, yet he remained quiet, placing his hands behind his head and focusing on the roof. Time passed with the soft murmuring of voices in the hall. Then Mason turned his head, piercing Mitch with a frown. "Come on, man. Let's forget the challenge list and go to a tittie bar."

Mitch shook his head. "Nope." He wouldn't back out now. They were running out of time, though. The ten o'clock deadline wasn't far away, and they still had three more challenges to complete. "Hurry up, Sean," Mitch raised his voice. "We don't have time for this."

"What's he doing?" Mason asked.

Blake shrugged. "Probably making plans for another round of masochism later."

Maree walked into the room, sparing them a shy smile before approaching the counter at the back of the room. Sean came in behind her, smirking, his face alight with mischief as he stopped beside Blake.

"Please tell me she didn't say yes," Mitch muttered. Mason would kill them if his perfect face turned up on magazines in a not-so-perfect fashion.

"Why's that?" Sean jerked his head in Mason's direction, his smile never faltering. "Look at the cocky bastard. He deserves a good dose of reality. And if she does do it, this will be the best night of my life."

Maree murmured questions to Mason, giving Mitch the opportunity to turn closer into Sean's body, so they wouldn't be overheard. "So she said yes?"

Sean continued to stare down at Mason who had his attention focused on the beautician. "Not entirely sure. She's worried about being fired, or sued, or publicly humiliated for defacing the flawless face of our fearless leader. But I'm kinda convincing when I wanna be."

"I bet you are," Blake muttered.

Mitch's chest started to pound as the woman shuffled back to the counter and ran a waxing stick around in the large warming tub. This wasn't right. Somewhere deep inside, under many layers of alcohol, Mitch's conscience was begging to be heard. Only the numerous glasses of beer and scotch seemed to be blocking the full force of the warning. He knew Mason deserved it. He couldn't wait to see the arrogant fucker's face when he looked in a mirror, but something else was nagging at him. Something that his drunken haze wouldn't let him figure out.

Oh, shit. Mitch bumped Sean's shoulder. "What about Saturday? Alana will kill me if Mason has one eyebrow in the wedding photos."

"Fuck," Blake breathed.

Sean's eyes widened. "I didn't think of that."

Mitch turned to the woman, poised to call her back into the hall. Too late. His heart sank to the soles of his feet. She'd already spread the pink gunk over Mason's left eyebrow—his entire eyebrow.

Holy mother of drunken misfortune, Alana was going to kill him. Then she would slaughter Mason for looking like an ass, Sean for instigating, Blake for letting it happen, and as usual, Ryan would be the golden child, let off scot free.

"What's with the frown?" Mason asked, snapping Mitch out of the bloodbath vision in his mind. Mason glanced from Maree, to Sean, then Mitch, and Blake, narrowing his eyes with each person, until he settled his gaze on Sean. "What the fuck have you guys done?"

"Nothin'." Sean shrugged. "Lay back and relax. Let the lovely lady do her job."

Mason glared. "If you've planned something, I'll fuck your shit up, Sean. You know I will." His mouth was set in a grim line as he closed his eyes again and rested his head back into the massage table.

Maree settled a shaky hand at one end of the dry wax, and tightened Mason's skin with the other. Her face was pale as she peered up at Sean for confirmation, then with one swift pull, the wax was gone.

"Motherfucker!"

CHAPTER 8

BLAKE PRESSED HIS LIPS TOGETHER, TENSING HIS STOMACH MUSCLES SO HE didn't break the deadly silence with a burst of laughter.

Mason lay still, his mouth agape, his eyes slowly blinking, while Mitch, Sean, Maree, and Blake stared at him, half in shock, half in contained hysterics. Well, there was no humor in the beautician's expression. The woman was pale, and he'd guess she was on the verge of losing her dinner.

Mason raised a hand and ran his fingers over the area where his left eyebrow used to be. "Call me paranoid, but why can I no longer feel my eyebrow?"

Maree cleared her throat and took a cautious step back.

"You can go now, sweetheart," Sean said, grinning.

"Wait. What?" Mason sat up. "What the fuck is going on?" His fingertips continued to rub the patch of red skin marking the line where the wax had been. "Give me a mirror."

Maree's bottom lip quavered. It was her own fault for being seduced by whatever lines Sean had given her, still, he felt sorry for the woman.

"Go." Blake jerked his head in the direction of the door. Truth was, he was kind of scared himself. With one eyebrow, Mason looked fucking ridiculous, which meant the guy would flip his lid in a big way.

"We'll take it from here," Blake added, sliding the door closed behind her as she scampered from the room.

"Give me a *god damn mirror*," Mason demanded. "If you've done what I think you've done, I'm going to break your face." He pushed from the table and grabbed the round mirror standing on the counter.

Mitch edged closer to the door, one eye trained on Mason who stared at his reflection. There was silence. Long, unending, silence that gave Blake goose bumps and made his heart pound harder. Any minute now Mason would crack. Any second, and he'd fly off the handle and—

"*You fuckin' asshole.*" Mason slammed the mirror down on the counter, turned and launched himself over the massage table, grabbing a laughing Sean around the neck. "You're dead."

Sean's laughter died on a grunt when Mason caught him in a head lock, bent him over, and landed a swift uppercut to the gut.

Ouch. Blake didn't move. One—he didn't want to attract attention, and two—Mason deserved a few seconds to alleviate his anger. This scene had played out before. The two of them would wrestle, throw a few soft blows in the stomach region, let out their aggression, and call it quits.

Mason raised his arm, cocked his fist and swung. High. *Oh, fuck.* That blow wasn't soft, and it definitely wasn't near the stomach. Sean's head snapped back, and they both fell to the floor in a mass of swinging arms and heaving chests.

"Grab him," Blake called to Mitch.

They approached, trying not to trip over the couple rolling along the linoleum, slamming equipment, and banging into walls.

"Thatshh enough," Mitch slurred with menace, appearing like a transvestite Dom with all his feminine make-up.

Mason and Sean continued to fight, their blows smacking harder, their grunts becoming louder.

"Shit. I'm going in," Mitch announced, and jumped on Mason's back, WWE champion style.

"Christ!" Blake shook his head at the school-yard scene. Mitch yanked at Mason's shoulders, giving Sean the distraction he needed to launch his fist at the singer's jaw. The crack echoed through the room, followed by a loud curse.

"Enough," Blake yelled.

They ignored him. Mason and Sean exchanged stomach and rib jabs while drunken Mitch rode Mason's back like a rodeo champion. The sliding door opened with a thwack, the brightness of the hall bathing them in light as the salon owner stormed into the doorway, Ryan positioned behind her.

"What are you doing?" she screeched.

The three "children" on the floor paused.

"Get out!"

Blake shook his head in disgust, and maybe a little humor, as Mitch raised his fake lashes and glanced sheepishly at the woman. Mason remained poised over Sean, one hand at his throat while the other was cocked, ready to strike.

"Come on, guys," Blake pleaded. "Let's move."

Mason glared at Sean, landing a final blow to the drummer's stomach before pushing to his feet and maneuvering around the lady as he strode from the room.

"Sorry, ma'am. It was my fault," Sean murmured, taking Mitch's offered hand and hauling himself up. "I'll give you my contact details, and you can bill me for any damages."

"Oh, I will," she growled, stepping back to let them into the hall.

Ryan trudged after Mason, then Sean and Mitch followed, leaving Blake with the fuming woman.

"I'm sorry—"

She cut him off with a firm shake of her head. "Leave."

He nodded and did as instructed, passing Sean at the front counter, before heading outside. The rest of the guys stood in a group out of the path of pedestrians, the bodyguards poised a few feet away, scanning the people who passed.

"It doesn't look that bad," Ryan offered, throwing Blake his baseball cap and handing Mitch and Mason theirs.

Mason snatched the cap with a raised eyebrow...well, the skin where his eyebrow should be, and rammed the cap low on his head. One of the bodyguards snorted and turned away, trying to cover his laughter with a fake cough.

"Don't you fucking start," Mason warned. "If any of you say a god damn word, it's on like Donkey Kong, you hear me? I hate you assholes."

"What did I do?" Ryan snapped. "You know what, for once, I think you deserve it. This might finally get your head out of your ass."

"Settle down." Blake placed the cap on his head and entered the makeshift circle, trying not to make eye contact with anyone. They resembled a group of misfits—Mason with his lopsided face, Mitch with his transvestite make-up, and Ryan with an unnatural fake tan that appeared bright orange in the glow of the Las Vegas night.

"Yeah, settle down, Oompa Loompa," Mason taunted, then turned his back to the group.

"You are so fucking childish," Ryan muttered. "And you can't even notice your ugly face with the cap on."

"It'll hide the disfigurement for tonight. What about tomorrow, and the next day?" Mason snarled. "What about the wedding, huh? Do you think it'll grow back overnight?"

The question went unanswered, the hustle of Las Vegas growing louder around them. Blake had no intention of announcing he thought it would take at least a month to grow back. He valued his life too much.

"What the hell happened to your spray tan, anyway?" Mitch asked Ryan. "You and Blake had the easiest treatments, but dude, you look like an orange Skittle."

"I chose the wrong color," Ryan muttered.

The beauty salon door opened with a soft squeak and they turned to watch Sean walk along the path toward them. His stride lacked confidence, and when he lifted his gaze, his face was blotchy with patches of red around his chin and right eye.

"Christ," Mitch whimpered. "Alana is going to cut my dick off."

Blake didn't doubt it. Tomorrow morning they had to catch the private jet back to New York so the happy couple could finalize the last of the wedding plans for the ceremony the following day. Ryan wasn't going to lose his tan overnight, and Sean's face would be covered in bruises by then.

The front pocket of Blake's jeans vibrated, and he stepped away from the group to reach for his phone. Alana's name displayed across the screen and he frowned, wondering why Mitch's fiancée would be calling.

"Hey, Allie. What's up?"

"Blake, is Gabi with you?"

What a way to kick-start his heart into overdrive. "No. Why? Where are you?" He turned back to the guys, making eye contact with Mitch.

"I'm at a strip club, a few blocks from the Bellagio. Gabi was upset and came outside for fresh air. I checked not long after, and she was still struggling with something. She said she needed a few minutes to compose herself. Now she's gone and won't answer her phone."

The blood drained from Blake's face, and Mitch stared at him in concern. "Why was Gabi upset?" he asked. It wasn't like his angel to walk off in the middle of a bachelorette party, and although she'd been quiet in the few hours they spent together since he returned from Richmond, he hadn't noticed anything out of the ordinary. She'd just seemed tired.

"She had an argument with Kate."

The few words were enough to send Blake into a panic. His fiancée didn't cause drama. If she'd had an argument with someone, she must've had good reason.

"Kate mentioned that you two hooked up, which upset Gab, but I'm certain that wasn't the main problem. She was emotional before that. I assumed it has to do with the two of you."

Fuck. He'd known Kate would be at the party, and he'd chickened out on telling Gabi about their past. Not that he'd had any real opportunity to tell her. He'd spent the last six days in Richmond with Mason, and although they spoke on the phone more than once a day, there hadn't been an appropriate moment to discuss previous conquests. Then when he got home, he only had time to dump his bags, repack fresh clothes, and leave for the airport again.

He couldn't fathom something wrong between the two of them. They didn't fight. They rarely argued, and he was thankful they were still in the smitten stage of their relationship. Everything Gabi did made him happy, and he'd assumed he did the same for her. Their few problems stemmed from Gabi's insecurities about other women, and again, she handled that with dignity and patience.

"Tell me where you are. I'm on my way." His words sparked the interest of his friends. They strode toward him, frowns of concern on each of their mangled faces.

"We're about to leave. She mentioned going back to the Bellagio, so why don't we both go there. We can meet at the start of the fountain."

"OK. I'm going to try calling her. I'll see you soon."

"All right," she replied, her tone soft. "I'm really sorry, Blake. I didn't think Kate would say something so stupid. We've all had too much to drink, and things got out of hand."

Blake clenched his fist. He could only imagine how bad Gabi was hurting. She'd already had to deal with his ex, Michelle. Then the attention his online video had given him. It seemed like every woman in the US now considered him a challenge to conquer.

"Don't worry about it." He made eye contact with Mitch and mouthed "I've gotta go." Then to Alana he said, "I'll meet you at the fountain."

He ended the call and let out the breath tightening his lungs. "I'm leaving."

"What's wrong?" Mitch asked. His eyes were still glazed from alcohol, his forehead creased in concern.

"They don't know where Gabi is. I need to find her."

"What do you mean, 'they don't know where she is'?" Ryan asked.

"She was upset or something. I don't know the full story. She took off and won't answer Alana's calls." He rubbed at his temples, trying to relieve the building pressure.

"What do you want us to do?"

Blake glanced over his shoulder, surprised to see concern in Mason's eyes. "Nothin'." He shook his head. "You guys continue without me. Hopefully I'll find her on the way to the hotel."

"No. I'm coming with you," Mitch said, following along beside him.

Ryan began walking. "I'll come too."

"You're not leaving me with Sean, so I'm tagging along," Mason added. "We can change ten dollars for pennies along the way and wipe that challenge from the list. We're running short on time."

Blake ignored the conversation. He didn't care what they did, or how many challenges they completed. All he cared about was Gabi. He pounded out the remaining steps to the street corner and turned onto the bustling South Las Vegas Boulevard. Mitch kept pace beside Blake as he scrolled through his phone and pressed on Gabi's contact details. The phone rang, once, twice, each ring increasing the rampant beat of his heart.

"Fuck." How was he going to find her in the Vegas crowd at night?

He tried again, hating the way Mitch watched him with concern. All it did was boost his own panic, and freaking out was the last thing he wanted to do.

Ring. Ring. Ring. No answer.

"We'll catch up with you," Mason spoke behind Blake.

Mitch turned. "Where are you going?"

"We'll cut across the road to Excalibur and organize the pennies."

"Fuck the pennies," Mitch answered. "Forget the challenges. We've all had enough of it anyway."

Mason clapped a hand on Mitch's shoulder causing him to fumble backward. "Bro, I lost an eyebrow. I'm not giving up now. We'll take one of the bodyguards, be in and out in two seconds, and catch up with you by the end of the block."

Mitch glanced at Blake, his friend's fake eyelashes fluttering amidst the horrific make-up. They were both thinking the same thing—Mason was going to freak when he found out the challenge for honeymoon rights were only created for Alana's benefit.

Blake shook his head, silently instructing Mitch not to bring it up. They could deal with the explosion later. "I'll be walking slowly to scan the crowd," he told Mason. "Catch up when you can, and keep an eye out for Gabi."

"Will do." Mason turned, jerking his head at Ryan and Sean to follow, then began walking in the opposite direction.

Blake stepped back from the flow of foot traffic and tried calling Gabi again. This time it rang twice before the phone connected, and his stomach clenched in relief.

"Blake."

His panic returned with her haunted tone. "Tell me where you are, angel, and I'll come get you."

She sniffed, and sucked in a ragged breath. Not even the heavy sound of people talking in the background disguised her crying. "I want to go home. I'm lost here. I'm confused. I need to leave."

Home. The single word petrified him. He knew she didn't mean their apartment in New York. He glanced at Mitch, unsure what the hell to do. What had Blake done to make her want to run away? "Come on, gorgeous, tell me where you are."

Her choked inhale carried through the phone line. "No. Stay with Mitch and have fun. I've already ruined Alana's night. I'll be OK. I just need time alone."

His heart stopped beating. He couldn't give her what she needed. He had to be by her side and couldn't fathom not running to her when she was upset. "Gabi, what's going on? Everything was fine a week ago. Is this about Kate? She means nothing to me. I don't want anyone else, you know that."

"It wasn't Kate. Or the thousands of other women vowing to take you away from me. But being drunk and emotional hasn't made that any easier to ignore. I'm struggling, Blake. I'm drowning."

"Angel, tell me where you are." He was losing his mind. His palms were sweating, his heart beating in erratic pulses, his throat dry. Gabi was the strong one. He'd never had to be her savior before. "Please, you're freaking me out. I need you to tell me where to find you."

"I'm near the Bellagio fountain. I lost my keycard to the hotel suite."

"Don't move." He broke out in a run, sliding past pedestrians, weaving in and out of the crowd. "I'm on my way."

CHAPTER 9

GABI LEANED AGAINST THE WAIST-HIGH CEMENT FOUNTAIN WALL, KEEPING her head downcast so the hundreds of passing people didn't pay her attention. She could've continued into the Bellagio and asked the receptionist for another room card, or gone back into the strip club with Alana, but talking to anyone was the last thing she wanted to do. Pretending her life was perfect wasn't an option anymore.

She needed to go home, back to Australia, to crawl into her childhood bed and pretend the week from hell hadn't happened. Yet in reality, leaving the man she loved was unthinkable. She only hoped Blake didn't look at her differently once he heard her news.

"You scared the hell out of me." His deep voice carried from in front of her, and she raised her gaze to meet his panicked raven stare. His chest heaved from exertion as he gripped her shoulders, dragging her into his body. She relaxed into him, resting her chin against his shoulder. Her eyes stung from unshed tears, and her chest grew heavy with sorrow. She ignored the unwanted emotions, clinging to the love in his embrace.

Mitch jogged into view, lowering a cell phone from his ear and placing it in his jacket pocket. Gabi frowned, blinking away the moisture in her vision while she tried to determine if the shadow from the lead guitarist's baseball cap was making her hallucinate. "What happened to Mitch's face?"

Blake's grip relaxed around her waist, and he peered over his shoulder. "Beauty salon challenge. He's covered in bridal make-up."

Gabi wanted to laugh at the drag queen standing before her, yet all she mustered was a smile.

Mitch slowed to a walk, stopping a foot behind Blake. "You OK, Gab?" His eyes held sympathy she couldn't handle. She turned her face away, nestling into Blake's shoulder as she wrinkled her nose to stem the tears. As arrogant and flirtatious as the men of Reckless Beat were, nothing came before the women they cared about. Even the single men knew the importance of the females that had joined the family.

"Talk to me," Blake spoke into her hair. "Tell me what's going on, and I'll fix it for you."

She closed her eyes and hugged him tight, loving him so much more with every breath. But he couldn't fix this. Nobody could.

"Can we go somewhere quieter?" she whispered.

"OK." He reached for her hand and let his other arm fall. He turned to face Mitch, exposing her to the attention of Mason, Ryan, and their two bodyguards who jogged up to meet them.

"You didn't have to take off without me," Sean huffed, shuffling up behind the group with his pockets stretched and pants riding low. "I can't run with this load full of shit in my pants."

Gabi's eyes widened, and a middle-aged woman strolling past paused with a gasp.

"Oh, come on, lady." Sean scowled at the offended stranger. "I didn't mean literally *shit*."

The woman's mouth gaped as she gave Sean a measured stare, and then continued to walk in a huff.

"Penny challenge," Blake muttered.

It made her smile that Mitch had gone to so much effort to make the night enjoyable for Alana...even though Gabi had now ruined it.

"Everything all right?" Mason asked.

"Yeah," Blake answered for her. "Gabi and I are going to find a quiet place to talk. We might catch up with you later."

Mason nodded and Blake led her forward, strolling around the corner of the fountain and into the Bellagio parking lot. He remained silent as they weaved in and out of cars and finally slowed when they reached a small patch of trees and grass on the other side.

"Is this OK?" he asked. "We can go back to the suite if you prefer."

"No." She shook her head. She didn't want to be suffocated by their hotel room. For the moment, she was happy to remain in the cool night air, even though the heavy bustle of traffic made it far from peaceful.

Blake leaned into one of the slim trees and reached for her hips, pulling her body into his. "Talk to me."

Gabi glanced over her shoulder, needing a few more moments to gather her thoughts, and found the Reckless Beat men, their bodyguards, and now Leah and Alana standing on the other side of the parking lot, watching.

She let out a defeated sigh.

"They're worried about you," Blake murmured. "So am I."

She lowered her gaze to Blake's grey shirt and nodded. She appreciated the concern, loved the support they gave, yet nothing eased the weight on her chest. Nothing soothed the torment.

"Why do you want to leave me, angel?"

His heartfelt question was her undoing. She sniffed back the emotion drowning her from the inside out and sucked in a breath. "I could never leave you."

"You said you wanted to go home."

She shook her head. Blake was her home—her strength. She glanced up at him and swiped the tears now rushing down her cheeks with the back of her hand. His dark irises were filled with sorrow. He was hurting for her, and his compassion made her ache all the more.

"Blake..." Her bottom lip quavered.

He raised his hand, cupped her cheek and pleaded with his eyes for her to continue.

"I—" How did she tell him about the pregnancy? She didn't know where to start. Couldn't fathom how he would react. They hadn't wanted a baby. Hadn't even discussed children yet. And that was only the beginning.

With another deep breath, the words fell from her numb lips. "The day you left for Richmond was the first time I'd been alone since relocating here. Before that, things had been moving too fast. I'd become so caught up in loving you and readjusting to my new life that I lost track of myself."

He frowned and tightened his hands around her hips. His strength borrowed under her skin, but didn't reach her broken heart.

"I didn't realize I was late." She paused, letting the statement sink in. When his frown deepened she squeezed her eyes shut, hating that she had to spell it out. "I found out I was pregnant."

"Gabi."

She blinked at the breathy way he whispered her name and found his eyes alight with happiness, the corners of his lips tilting. Excitement emanated from him in gushing waves, drowning her, stealing her breath. She'd been happy when she found out, too. Happy, yet more scared than she'd ever been in her life.

"No." She shook her head and winced at the pain that built in her chest. "Don't."

The cheer vanished from his features, and he reached for her hand, squeezing it between his. "Tell me."

She tightened her grip on his fingers and stared at his hand, frowning at the black paint on his nails. Another result of the beauty salon, she assumed. "I searched the phone book and made some calls to get an appointment with a local doctor. I didn't know who to pick and ended up going to a man willing to see me that day," she continued, running the tips of her finger over his smooth nail polish. "He confirmed my assumptions. Even sent me for blood tests to determine how far along I was."

The image of the doctor's smile was still vivid in her mind. *"Congratulations,"* he'd said. *"You're going to be a mom."* The words had stopped her heart and made it swell, all in an instant.

Blake's Adams apple bobbed with a deep swallow. "Go on," he murmured.

She straightened her shoulders, and looked him in the eye. "Seven weeks pregnant." The words restricted her throat. "Seven weeks, and I'd had no clue I'd been carrying our child."

Blake's gaze searched hers with confusion.

"Three days later the baby was gone. I had a miscarriage."

His lips parted as his shoulders slumped. "Oh, angel." He pulled her into his chest, surrounding her in the warmth of his arms, and held her tight.

"I'm so sorry."

She leaned into his strength and let the emotions she'd been holding in run free—the pain, the loneliness, the guilt, the heartache. It poured from her in chest-heaving sobs, her tears dampening his shirt, her hands running around his back to hold him close.

She hadn't contemplated having a child, yet now that it was gone, she found it hard to breathe. In three days, she'd envisaged their entire future. The colors they would decorate the nursery. The sweet smell of a newborn. Their toddler's first steps. Bright smiles and warm cuddles. All of it came and went in the blink of an eye. And now all she had left was consuming grief.

"Why didn't you tell me?" he asked. "I would've come home. I would've been by your side as fast as the jet could get me back to you."

She nodded, and sucked in a wavering breath. "I know. When I found out I was pregnant, I didn't want to tell you over the phone. I wanted to see your face. I wasn't entirely convinced you'd think it was good news." She leaned back and studied his glazed eyes. "We haven't spoken about children. I needed to witness your reaction. I needed to be sure you wouldn't resent me."

"I'd never resent you, angel." He swept a hand through her hair, wiping away the stray strands that stuck to her cheeks. "I love you," he murmured against her cheek. "I love you so much. I'm sorry I wasn't there when you needed me." He continued to bathe her in comforting words, hugging her until her sobs turned into whimpers and her whimpers faded into the night.

When she had the strength to meet his gaze again, his eyes were filled with pain. Guilt haunted her for putting it there. She'd wanted to keep the news to herself, at least until after the wedding. Mitch and Alana meant a lot to them both. Sharing this with them, when they were celebrating the start of their marriage, was a burden Gabi didn't want to bear.

"Deep down, I knew that, but my mind hasn't been rational lately. The doctor told me it was due to the hormonal changes in my body." She nestled back into his chest, hiding her face from view. "And after the miscarriage, I feared you wouldn't want me anymore." Her eyes began to burn, and a fresh wash of tears trailed down her cheeks.

Not only had she lost their child, she'd been hysterical thinking she would lose Blake too. If he had his heart set on a large family, and her body couldn't provide it, what use was she to him?

"What?" He grabbed her shoulders, softly pushing her back to meet his harsh features.

"I'm a wreck, Blake. What happens if I can't carry a baby to term? You have women flocking after you, and you'd be stuck with someone who can't give you children."

This was why she wanted the peace of Australian starlit skies and fresh Queensland air. She was irrational, crazy with grief, and unable to determine if her thoughts were justified or hormone induced.

"Gabi." He lowered his face so they were nose to nose. "You're killing me." His throat convulsed with a swallow, and the glaze in his eyes made her want to crumble to her knees. "Please don't do this to yourself. I don't care about kids. I don't care about other women. There's only one thing I need for the rest of my life, and that's you." He brushed his lips against hers, then pulled her back into his chest. "I only need you, angel."

CHAPTER 10

Mitch stood alongside Alana, watching Gabi crumple into Blake's arms. His fiancée mentioned the rift Kate caused in the strip club, yet what he was witnessing was far more emotional than a woman with insecurities over past conquests.

"Kate and your mom both sent me a text message," Leah murmured. "They made it back to their rooms safely."

"Great." Alana didn't tear her gaze from Gabi.

He was annoyed that the bachelorette party hadn't gone the way he planned. Only it pained him more to see his fiancée worried for the woman who had become one of her closest friends. Gabi was a part of the Reckless family, and when one of them was hurting, they all did. Not that Allie currently acknowledged his existence. He was ninety-nine percent sure her lack of physical contact and rigid posture were because she was holding in her wrath over the way the guys looked.

"Shit!" Mason broke the silence. "It's five to ten." Without warning, the Reckless Beat front man threw his jacket to the ground, and began working the buttons of his shirt.

"What the hell are you doing?" Sean asked.

"Someone has to do the fucking nude run. We have less than five minutes."

Mitch suppressed a grin, remaining quiet while Mason shucked his shoes and yanked down his pants.

"Jesus Christ," Leah gasped and turned her back to Mason. "I don't get paid enough to put up with this crap."

"I didn't lose a friggin' eyebrow for nothing." Mason's clothes hit the pavement and seconds later he was running away from them, heading toward the Bellagio fountain in nothing but a baseball cap.

The bodyguards swore, glancing at each other, and then stared after Mason's retreating form in panic.

"Go." Mitch jutted his chin. "He'll need all the protection he can get." The rest of the group were fine to hang around unguarded in the parking lot. Nobody was paying them attention.

"I've gotta get this on camera." Sean took his cell out of his pocket and took off after them, the pennies weighing down his pockets jingling in protest.

Mitch shook his head and turned his gaze back to Blake and Gabi. He should probably leave, too, and give them privacy, yet he couldn't convince himself to walk away.

"I should've mentioned this before Mason ran his naked ass past," Leah said, her tone devoid of remorse. "We didn't complete all our challenges."

"Don't worry," Mitch chuckled. "I was happy to keep my mouth shut about not getting the butterfly tattoo."

"Yeah," Ryan shrugged. "And I kinda paid the waitress when I was meant to dine and ditch."

Mitch burst into laughter. "You idiot. I knew you would."

"Yeah, he's the idiot," Alana muttered, taking a step away.

His laughter faltered, becoming fake. His fiancée was going to stab him. He was only thankful that she didn't seem eager to do it in public.

"Well why didn't you do it yourself?" Ryan scowled. "You know I'm a soft touch."

"For that exact reason. I didn't want to walk out without paying either."

Their laughter died into uncomfortable silence, and long moments passed as they watched Blake and Gabi on the other side of the parking lot.

"I feel helpless," Alana murmured.

"It could be nothing," Leah offered. "Gabi had a lot to drink. Hell, we all did. I still can't walk properly. And Blake's been away for a week. She might've missed having him around."

Alana shook her head. "No. Gabi's not like that."

Mitch grasped her shoulder, wordlessly offering support. She shrugged off the touch until his hand fell back to his sides. Not good. Not good at all. He chose to ignore the imminent threat of an argument, hoping with tipsy optimism that her barely contained fury would simmer by the time they reached their suite. "Blake wouldn't placate her over something inconsequential, either. They both look upset. My guess is, something major has happened."

"Like what?" Leah asked.

Mitch shrugged. That was the worst part. Even in his buzzed state, he could sense the seriousness of the situation. Only he had no clue what it was about. "I'm not sure. We'll have to wait and see."

•••

Gabi's warmth left Blake's body as she stepped back from their embrace. He reached for her hand, still craving her touch, and entwined their fingers. Talk about blindsided. He hadn't seen this coming. If given a thousand guesses, he wouldn't have come close.

Pregnant.

Miscarriage.

The words made his mouth dry. And she'd gone through it alone. He hadn't even noticed the change in their phone conversations. What kind of a fiancé did that make him?

A commotion sounded near the pathway leading into the parking lot, and Gabi turned toward the noise. He followed her gaze, finding Sean loping toward Mitch, Alana, Leah, and Ryan, with a huge grin on his face.

Next, Mason sprinted into view, naked, holding his junk in his hands. The only thing concealing his identity was a baseball cap. The bodyguards followed close behind, stopping at the group while Mason yanked his clothes off the ground and rushed to hide between two parked SUV's.

"Please tell me I didn't just get an eye full of Mason's ass," Gabi asked, tilting her face up to meet his gaze.

Blake wrinkled his nose. "I didn't need to see that either."

She let out a breath of laughter that warmed his heart, and stared up into his eyes. "Life is never boring when I'm with you."

He gave an apologetic smile. For once, he hated the excitement in his life. Every time there was drama, it affected Gabi the worst. "Are you ready to speak to the others?"

She turned her focus back to his friends, her forehead creasing in concern. "Do we have to do this now?"

"No, angel." He squeezed her fingers, wishing like hell he could take away her pain. "We can do it whenever you're ready, but they're gonna be worried until they find out what's wrong."

Gabi inhaled deep, letting it out gradually. "OK. Let's get this over with."

He stared at her, helpless, entirely lost. Sucking up his own self-pity, he led her forward, stepping from the soft grass onto the asphalt.

"Wait." She planted her feet.

He didn't push her, simply ran his hand around her neck and kissed her temple, breathing in her scent, willing his love to soothe her. "We don't have to do this now. We can go back to our room. I'll call Mitch later."

"No. I want to get this over with. I just can't say the words." Her pleading eyes glanced up at him, the skin surrounding them now swollen and red. "Can you tell them?"

"Of course." It was the least he could do. He ran a finger along her jaw, lifting her chin so their gazes collided. His lips moved closer, kissing away the drying tears on her cheeks. "I'll do whatever you need me to do, angel."

They strode forward as one, his legs heavy, and his heart hollow. He ignored Mason who cautiously peeked out from between the cars and followed behind them to the group. Blake's mind was a mess, his emotions switching from the devastation of not being with Gabi when she needed him, to the pain of losing a child.

Their child.

A tiny baby.

Fuck. He still couldn't believe it.

Months ago, he'd been surrounded by friends, but lost in his own solitude. He'd never been whole until he met Gabi. And without them knowing, they'd almost started a family. Clenching his jaw, he breathed through his nose until the burn from his eyes faded. This was his time to be strong. The moment he'd been waiting for—to be a rock for the woman who'd always been his strength. He raised his chin, ignored his own selfish feelings, and closed the distance to the other band members.

"Everything OK?" Alana's soft voice asked.

Blake glanced at Gabi, wanting to make sure she wanted to continue. She gave a sad smile, nodded, and then broke eye contact to focus on her shoes.

"Not really." He met Alana's gaze and cleared his throat, dislodging the emotions trying to choke him. "Gabi had a miscarriage."

Leah gasped. Alana covered her mouth with a hand, and more than one person swore. For long heartbeats the unsightly group stood speechless, the heavy sound of traffic and distant chatter filling the void.

"I'm so sorry." Leah stepped forward, pulling Gabi into her arms.

Blake let his hand fall to his side, instantly missing the touch of her fingers against his. He watched Leah hold his fiancée, murmuring words in her ear, kissing her cheek. When she stepped back, she pierced him with a look of anguish. "If you need anything, please ask."

Blake gave a jerky nod. He didn't need anything, other than Gabi's happiness, and only time would bring that back to him. Alana moved closer, offering comfort. Gabi remained strong, hiding her pain under the sad smile she used too well. As the women talked in hushed voices, Mitch stepped toward Blake, preparing for a man hug. Blake retreated, putting his palms up to halt this friend. He couldn't handle sympathy right now. He couldn't do the whole, let's-hug-and-make-it-better scene. "I'm cool."

Mitch scrutinized him for long moments, getting under his skin, ramping his pulse. Then finally he inclined his head. "Let me know if you want to talk."

Blake stood frozen, thankful for the reprieve as Mitch moved on to hug Gabi. "We're all here for you," he spoke loud enough for Blake to hear. "Whatever you need, OK?"

Gabi nodded and pulled back to stare up at the lead guitarist. "What happened to your face?"

Her tone held a hint of humor that soothed the ache in Blake's chest.

This woman was far stronger than he was. Even lost in sadness, she could find happiness.

Mitch batted his fake lashes and puckered his glossy red lips. "Do you like?"

She chuckled, it was half-hearted and strained, but it was still laughter that warmed Blake's soul. He noticed his friends relax, their posture no longer stiff and awkward. None of them were used to women problems. Hell, none of them were used to long term women. With the addition of Alana, and now Gabi, the last year had been a steep learning curve for them all.

"It's different," she replied, smiling. "Maybe bright red isn't your color."

Mitch puffed out a laugh and gave Gabi a quick kiss to the forehead. "I'll go with a lighter shade next time."

"Move outta my way, woman." Mason shouldered Mitch out of the way. "It's my turn."

Mitch stumbled backward, moving to the side and allowing Mason to stand before Gabi. "How are you, sweetheart?"

Gabi shrugged. "I'm getting there."

She was a trooper. It must be in the Aussie blood because Blake sure as shit wasn't that strong.

"I had no clue you two were trying for kids." Mason stepped into her, wrapping his arms around her shoulders.

"We weren't."

Blake wanted to soothe the wince that crossed his fiancées face. "She found out about the pregnancy while I was in Richmond. And miscarried a few days later. She didn't want to tell me over the phone."

"Fuck," Mason muttered. "And you were in Richmond because of me. Christ. I'm so sorry."

"It's nobody's fault," Gabi whispered.

"Please, Gab," Mason started, then turned his gaze to Blake. "And you too, B. I may not seem like the caring type, but I've got a good set of shoulders if you need someone to lean on."

Blake couldn't reply. He was speechless. Instead, he concentrated on the loose stones in the parking lot asphalt, toeing them with his boot. He needed to be alone with Gabi. He needed to do something, *anything*, to take away the heaviness dragging him down.

"Please don't make me cry again." Gabi whimpered. "And what happened to your face?"

Blake's attention snapped to the slight smile tilting Gabi's lips.

The gentle comfort left Mason's features, and a frown settled in its place "Ask Sean," he muttered, stepping back into their group of friends.

Gabi shuffled sideways, leaning into Blake. "What happened to his eyebrow?" she muttered under her breath.

"I'll fill you in later."

Sean stepped forward next, and Gabi's mouth gaped. Mason had done some damage—a fat lip, swollen eye, and the bruising around Sean's jaw was darkening by the minute.

Gabi shook her head. "I'm not even going to ask, OK?"

"Good decision." He pulled her into his arms. "I'm sorry for your loss."

"Thank you."

Sean moved out of her arms, and Ryan slid in front of her. "Yes, I'm orange," he blurted. "Let's hope it washes off." Gabi chuckled and stepped into his opened arms, resting her head against his shoulder. "My heart's breaking for the both of you," he murmured into her hair. "If either of you need anything, you know we're all here for you."

Ryan let her go, allowing Blake to run his hand around her waist and pull her back into his side. The group murmured amongst themselves, the fun from the evening eviscerated. Blake rubbed his sternum, trying to alleviate the throb underneath his ribs while Gabi's plea from earlier repeated on a continuous loop in his head. Her instinct had been to go home, to leave him, and that hurt almost as much as witnessing her grief.

He didn't want her to find comfort elsewhere. He needed to be her strength. He wanted to be all she ever needed, like she was for him.

"What's wrong?" Gabi tilted her face to meet his gaze, her blue eyes sad yet resilient.

"I need to do something," he spoke to himself. He needed to make a difference, to start the healing process, and strengthen their relationship. Most of all, he had to occupy his mind with his love for her, so he didn't crumple in front of his friends.

"Like what?"

He stared into the distance, working ideas over in his head. The thought of losing her clawed at him. He hadn't been there for her, or their child. He'd been out of town, something he'd have to do more of in the future, with tours and promo obligations. She'd already suffered too much because of their love. First Michelle and his own stupidity, now this. She'd given up her country, her job, her family, and nothing would ever show her how grateful he was. But still, he needed to do something. He had to make a gesture that reaffirmed how much she meant to him.

He needed to place a ring on her finger.

"Marry me, angel," he murmured, turning into her.

She pulled back, frowning.

"I don't want to wait," he continued, knowing the months spent planning a proper wedding would be too long. He wanted another ring on her finger. He wanted her commitment in his heart. "I need you to be my wife. Now. Tonight."

"Why?" Her words lacked excitement, her gaze devoid of enthusiasm. "Why now?"

He gripped her hips, trying not to add to her problems by showing how much he needed this. "Because I don't want you to think leaving me is an option. I don't want you to ever turn to someone else for support. Let me show you how much I love you. How much I need you. I'm not trying to take your pain away. Nothing will fix what you've lost—"

"*We've* lost, Blake."

He nodded. "Yes." They both lost a child, but he felt like it was a burden she was carrying alone. He didn't know how to mourn something he never had. He didn't know if the torture consuming him was an overreaction when the idea of a baby had come and gone in the blink of an eye. All he knew was that it stung like a bitch, and it was nothing in comparison to what Gabi would be going through.

"What we've lost," he repeated. "I just need you to be mine. And I need to be yours."

She continued to stare at him, the silence around them beginning to penetrate. He broke eye contact for a moment and noticed their friends focused on them, waiting for an answer.

His eyes began to burn, and he squeezed them shut, dropping a hand from Gabi's waist to rub them with his thumb and forefinger. He sucked in a breath and winced as it shuddered on an exhale. *Fuck.* He was such a weak prick. He needed to man the hell up. Only, seeing Gabi like this was his undoing.

"Blake?" Gabi's hands came to rest on his chest, the warmth of her palms permeating his heart.

He opened his eyes and would've given every cent he had to see happiness in her beautiful eyes. "Please don't look at me like that," he begged. "If those fuckers see me cryin' they'll never let me live it down."

It was a lie. The guys knew better than to tease him over something like this. Making Gabi smile had been his objective. And thankfully, it worked.

"You'd cry for me, Blake?"

Her words were meant in jest, only they had the opposite effect, turning the vice on his chest tighter. "I'd cry a river if it meant you'd be happy."

Gabi's gaze swept over his face, back and forth, reading him, penetrating deep. "You always make me happy."

He cupped her jaw in his hands and leaned in so their breath mingled. "Then marry me. Be my wife."

GABI POSITIONED HERSELF BEFORE THE DOORWAY LEADING INTO THE AISLE OF the Las Vegas chapel. Her heart pounded, and her head spun as she clung to the colorful blooms Alana purchased on the way here.

Hours earlier, she'd been devastated, unsure what the future would hold once she told Blake about the baby. Would he be angry that she'd fallen pregnant? Would he be worried she couldn't give him a family later on? She certainly was. But no, he'd held her close and reaffirmed his love and devotion. Strengthening her with his compassion.

She should've known that was what he'd do. And although the pain hadn't subsided, he'd cleared her mind, helping her to resolve the hormonal insecurities, while sharing her suffering. The grief that stemmed from losing a newly conceived baby was hard to explain. She hadn't been blessed with feeling her child kick from inside her, or the blurred images of an ultrasound. She hadn't had anything physically within her grasp to lose, yet the concept of that baby was enough to tear her apart.

Blake seemed to understand that, and no words could express her gratitude. He completed her, making the hardships in her life bearable, turning the hurt into love, and the love into something that went beyond words. Marrying him was exactly what she wanted to do, and not even having her parents miss this special occasion would make her second guess her decision.

As soon as she'd said "yes," they'd rushed to the Marriage License Bureau, arranged the forms they needed, and with Leah's help, found a wedding chapel still open at midnight.

Apart from loved ones back home, Gabi was surrounded by people who had become her closest friends—her adopted family. Leah, Alana, and Mitch sat in the first pew to the left of the aisle, while Sean, Mason, and Ryan were on the right, with the two bodyguards remaining in the foyer.

Up until this moment, her life with Blake had been hectic, a roller-coaster of emotions. Yet right here, right now, it was quiet, relaxed, almost an eerie calm that cemented her confidence in marrying the man of her dreams.

Blake stood tall at the front of the chapel, his shoulders straight, his grin wide with warmth as he chatted with his friends. He was gorgeous. He always would be, and once they left here tonight, he'd forever be hers. She knew that now. No matter how many women tried to seduce him, or how many times they argued, Blake would always stay true to her.

Her smile widened as she stole silent moments to watch him. She adored everything her man had to offer—his compassion, the way his spiked raven hair stood out at humorous angles, the grin that melted her panties, and most of all, his love. Then his body turned toward her, and he stiffened.

She couldn't tear her gaze away. She never could. Even if she lived to be a hundred and five, her lifetime would never be long enough with this man. Never long enough spent under the captivating spell of his dark irises, or memorizing the designs of his deliciously inked skin.

He was made for her.

She took her first step into the room, then another, bringing herself closer to contentment. Each movement propelled her toward the only man who would ever bring her happiness. Silence reigned around them, the gazes of their friends making her self-conscious, but she didn't falter, didn't waver her gaze from Blake and the admiration in his eyes.

When she reached the head of the aisle, he held out his hand, welcoming her with an appreciative stare. Without pause, she entwined their fingers, leaving her bouquet to fall limp in her free hand. Warmth radiated from him as he tugged her forward, wrapping his arm around her waist and bringing them chest to chest.

"You look gorgeous," he murmured. His mouth found hers for a brief brush of lips before he pulled back to stare down at her.

"Thank you." The strapless gown was another purchase Alana had helped make on the way to the chapel. The top was a delicate bodice of crystal beads and glittered thread with the white satin material falling like a curtain from her waist. Simple yet elegant. Around her neck sat the white gold necklace Blake gave her for her birthday, the charms a constant reminder of the bond they shared. And on her feet were the red stiletto heels she'd worn to the bachelorette party. They didn't match her outfit in the slightest, and she didn't care. This was a ceremony about love and a commitment of forever. Style played no part, especially if you took note of Mason's solitary eyebrow, Mitch plastered with bridal make-up, Ryan's orange glow, and Sean's busted face.

"Are you ready?" A voice spoke from behind Blake.

Gabi glanced over his shoulder, finding a middle-aged man waiting for them, his smile warm and friendly.

"I've been ready for years," Blake replied, still having the ability to make her tingle from head to toe.

"OK, then, let's get you two married."

•••

Blake stared at Gabi, vaguely hearing the words of the marriage ceremony drift through his consciousness. He didn't care about the official words, they meant nothing to him. They weren't personalized to encompass the way he felt about the flawless woman before him. They didn't show an ounce of the emotion he held for her. They were merely the necessary sentences to make them man and wife. And *that* was what they both needed.

"Would you like to recite your own vows?" the man whispered.

Blake grinned at Gabi's wide-eyed expression and raised his chin. "I'll say my own."

"But..." Gabi's mouth worked as she glanced from Blake to the marriage official and back again. "I haven't prepared any."

"Don't worry, angel." He lifted their entwined fingers to his lips and kissed her knuckles. "You can repeat the traditional vows."

Her brow furrowed, but she gave a soft nod. "OK."

"Great. I'll get you started, Mr. Kennedy. Please repeat after me, I, Blake Kennedy, take you Gabrielle Smith, to be my wife."

Blake's cheeks lifted, and his heart did the biggest fucking flip of his life. A year ago, hell, even a few months ago, he never thought he'd be the happiest man in the world, standing tall in a dodgy Vegas chapel, smiling at the only woman he would ever love.

"I, Blake Kennedy, take you, Gabrielle Smith, to be my wife." He inhaled, filling his lungs with the sweet floral fragrance of her hair. God, he adored that scent. God, he adored her. "I didn't know happiness until I found you. I didn't know love until your lips brushed mine. And I'll never go another day without you in my life. You are everything to me. *Everything*, Gabi."

A feminine sniffle came from the first pew. He ignored it, empowered by the way his angel beamed back at him. "I promise I'll die still trying to make you as happy as you've made me."

"You make me happy," she whispered.

There was a pause of silence before the official spoke, "If you'll repeat after me, Gabi. I, Gabrielle Smith, take you, Blake Kennedy, to be my husband."

Gabi squeezed Blake's hand and inhaled a shaky breath. "I, Gabrielle Smith, take you, Blake Kennedy, to be my husband."

"To share the good times, and the hard times, side by side," the official continued.

Gabi glanced at the man, then back up at Blake. "No." She shook her head, and Blake's legs weakened. *Was she backing out of the ceremony already?*

"I'll do my own."

"Shit, Gabi," Blake muttered. "Don't scare me like that."

Her lips widened with the most dazzling, brilliantly beautiful smile.

"Blake, you're my strength, my peace, my everything. And even though I regret not thinking about vows until two minutes ago, I want you to know that you mean the world to me. I can't imagine waking up every morning without your cheeky smile to brighten my day. You complete my life. You make me whole, and I promise to never take you for granted."

She glanced over her shoulder, smiling at their friends, then turned back to him, her eyes glassy with forming tears. "You've given me a new family, and one day—" she faltered, her smile fading as her lips trembled. "And one day," she puffed out a breath and squared her shoulders. "I hope we can make one of our own."

Christ. A knife stabbed through his chest, hard and unyielding. He'd had a tough life—shitty parents, poverty, drug addiction, yet nothing was harder to bear than watching Gabi suffer. He circled her waist with his free hand, not giving a shit that he squashed her flowers when he pulled her into his body. She sunk into him, her cheek resting against his shoulder.

The official cleared his throat, and Blake met his questioning gaze. "Would you like me to give you a moment?"

"No." Gabi shook her head. "Please continue."

"Who has the rings?"

"I do," Blake answered, pulling them from his pocket and holding them out in the palm of his hand. Gabi leaned back and smiled as she reached for the white gold ring he'd picked for himself. They were temporary pieces, both costing less than a grand, and nowhere near good enough to adorn Gabi's hand. But they would do for tonight.

"Blake, as you place the ring on Gabi's finger, please repeat after me."

Blake lifted her soft hand in his, positioning her ring at the tip of her trembling wedding finger. For the first time in an hour, his heart was pounding for reasons other than pain. Her smile, the one that came freely, without sorrow, spread across her face, and he grinned back at her in disbelief. This woman, this perfect, adorable, strong willed, hearted, and minded woman, was about to be his. For life.

"I give you this ring as a symbol of my love and devotion," the official stated.

Blake cleared his throat and peered into Gabi's eyes as he repeated. "I give you this ring as a symbol of my love and devotion." He slid the ring to the top of her finger, thankful that it fit perfectly. "I will always be faithful. I will always put your needs before mine, and I will never stop loving you."

"Gees, someone's getting carried away," Mason interrupted.

Blake shook his head with a laugh, and chuckles echoed from the front pew. He couldn't help getting carried away. He wanted Gabi to know what she meant to him, even though no amount of words would ever achieve that.

"I think it's sweet," Gabi murmured.

"Your turn, Gabi. Please repeat after me."

She copied what Blake had done, placing his ring at the top of his finger and didn't wait for the official before reciting the words. "I give you this ring as a symbol of my love and devotion."

His stomach tilted, somersaulted, fucking convulsed while she slid the ring into place, making them husband and wife.

"Nothing will ever come between us," she continued.

Blake clutched her hand, squeezing it tight as he smiled at her, waiting impatiently for the official to finish reciting the marriage declaration. He wanted to get her out of here and into his bed. This time though, it wasn't for fooling around. She told him intimacy wouldn't be possible for a while, but he needed to hold her, to entwine their legs, stare into her eyes and run his hands through her smooth hair.

"Blake and Gabrielle, marriage is the clasping of hands, the bending of hearts, and the union of two lives as one. Your marriage must stand, not by the authority of the state, nor by the words of the marriage official, but by the strengths of your love and the power of faith in each other. May your marriage be consumed with love and happiness, and your lives together filled with patience, tolerance and understanding."

Gabi's smile spread, lifting her cheeks, brightening her eyes. She clung to his hand, squeezing his fingers tight as she bit her lip.

"Ladies and gentlemen, Gabrielle and Blake have declared before all of us that they will live together in marriage. They have made special promises to each other. They have symbolized it by joining hands, taking vows and exchanging rings. I, therefore, declare Blake and Gabrielle to be husband and wife. Are you ready for your first kiss as a married couple?"

Blake's palms began to sweat.

"You better believe it," Gabi announced, untwining their fingers to clutch the front of his shirt. She pulled him close, grinning even though a lone tear streaked her cheek.

He chuckled, placing his mouth against hers, trying to kiss life back into her soul. He gripped her hips, lifting her off the ground and continued to savor her lips while he carried her higher. A wolf whistle split the air with cheers, laughter, and applause.

He was married. He had a fucking gorgeous wife. And for the rest of his life—no, even in death, there would never be another woman for him.

CHAPTER 12

MITCH FOCUSED ON ALANA'S ASS AS SHE STORMED AHEAD, KEEPING HER distance along the hotel hallway. She'd been silent since the end of the ceremony, and he'd kind of hoped it was because she was upset over Gabi and Blake's loss. Nope. She was pissed off, and no matter how hot she looked in those fuck me boots and her thigh-high dress, there was no way he was getting laid again tonight.

"It was a nice wedding, don't ya think?" he called out, wanting to know the degree of her anger before they entered the confined space of their suite.

"Yeah," she snarled.

Blake and Gabi had retreated to the hotel after the wedding, and Leah had retired for the night. So Mitch followed his fiancée back to the Bellagio for some naked play. Only now he second guessed his decision. Maybe he should've gone to the strip club with Mason and Sean after all.

His sweet and innocent Allie was furious.

Up ahead, she opened the suite door with the swipe of the room card and went inside, not bothering to hold it open for him. She would've left him standing in the hall if he hadn't jammed his foot into the doorway in time.

"What's your problem?" he asked, storming inside, letting tiredness and the waning alcoholic buzz fuel his frustration. It wasn't as if he had any control over the stupid shit his friends did.

She paused in front of the kitchenette and turned on her heels. "What's my problem?" She placed her hands on her hips, squaring her shoulders. That was the exact moment when Mitch realized how much shit he was in.

"*What's my problem?* We're getting married in," she glanced at her dainty silver watch, "less than forty hours, and after what you and your stupid friends did tonight, I'm going to have to stand at the altar with a fiancé who is accompanied by dumb and fucking-dumber. Not to mention Ryan, who looks like the spokesman for Fanta."

Yep…he was in a whole heap of trouble. When Alana dropped an f-bomb, it was usually a good sign that he needed to back the hell up.

"Sean's face is covered in bruises. And Mason…" She frowned and threw her hands up in the air. "He has one eyebrow. *One eyebrow, Mitch!*" Alana shook her head in disgust, turned and stormed toward their bedroom.

He began following her, and then stopped when she slammed the door. "Yeah, OK, so I guess I'll sleep on the couch."

She didn't answer.

Fuck this. It wasn't his fault Sean and Mason were childish pricks. He never wanted to do those stupid challenges in the first place. This was Leah's fault. She should answer to the fury, not him.

He strode to the bedroom door, flung it open and stalked to Alana who stood near the head of the bed, reaching behind her back to undo her dress. "This isn't my fault, *sugar*," he snarled. "I have no control over what those assholes do. And I'm sorry the wedding won't be perfect like you imagined, but that's tough shit."

She jerked back. "Tough shit? Nice, Mitchell, real nice. I've spent too many long hours and sleepless nights planning our special day to shrug and say 'oh well'." She shook her head and turned her back to him. "I can't believe you."

"Why are you so worried?"

"Are you serious?" she swung around and got in his face.

He pressed his lips together, using every ounce of his intoxicated restraint so he didn't burst into laughter. It didn't matter how angry she became, his woman would always look innocent to him. Such a sweet face contorted with lines of rage was all kinds of funny.

"The world is going to see our wedding photos. Not only my family and friends. Not just your crazy band members. The entire human race will be judging us."

"So? Who gives a shit?"

Her eyes widened. "Mitchell!"

"What, honey?"

Her mouth gaped and this time he couldn't hold in the grin that took over his face. She was too damn cute, and his dick had taken notice. "As long as you and I are happy, who cares about anyone else?" he asked, stepping forward, bringing them toe to toe.

She stared up at him, releasing a sigh as the harshness faded from her features. "Mason has one eyebrow."

A laugh burst from him and slowly a smile lifted her lips. "It isn't funny, Mitchell."

"Yeah," he chuckled. "It really is." He grabbed her waist and pulled her into his body. "You should've seen his face when he found out the beautician had waxed it off. It was epic."

"Well, I hope it was worth it." She pushed at his shoulders, and he held tight, not letting her leave. "Because you're going to look like a complete jackass standing at the front of the church with his lopsided face."

Mitch shrugged. "They'll make me look better."

She pushed again. "No, they won't." She wiggled in his arms, grunting in frustration.

"Where are you trying to go in such a hurry?"

"I'm tired and grumpy." *As if he hadn't noticed.* "I want to have a shower and go to bed."

"I've got something to relieve your anger," he ground his pelvis against hers, enjoying the way his balls tightened with the friction.

She stopped struggling and glared. "Don't even go there." She gave another violent push and with reluctance, he let her go.

She wanted to get laid as much as he did. He could see it in the way her gaze stalked him from the corner of her eyes, and the slow way she sauntered to the end of the bed, just out of reach, to seductively pull the straps of her dress down.

"Don't taunt me, woman."

She glanced over her shoulder—her eyebrows raised in defiance—and continued to let the dress fall into a puddle of material at her feet.

"Keep going. You'll soon find yourself flat on your back with my cock buried deep inside you."

"I said I wasn't in the mood." She focused on the shiny black leather of her boots, lifting one foot to the mattress and gradually lowering the zipper.

Wasn't in the mood, my ass. Mitch strolled around the bed, and moved in behind her, letting the hardness pressing against his zipper nudge her butt. She stiffened, one boot covered foot still poised on the mattress.

He bent over her, positioning his mouth at her ear. "You're a liar." He ran his fingers along her spine, loving the way her body shuddered when he gripped the base of her neck. "A pretty little liar."

She released a barely audible whimper.

"You know how I can tell?" He trailed his free hand over her bottom, underneath the thin lace of her G-string. With a bite to her earlobe, he cupped the heat between her thighs, sliding two fingers through the slickness of her pussy. "Because you're soaking wet."

She squirmed, trying with minimal conviction to dislodge his hand.

"Keep grinding against me, Allie." He reached higher on her neck, pulling the hair at the base of her skull. "The more you grind, the hotter I get."

She mewled, thrusting back into him, sinking his fingers deep into her heat. The way she clamped down around him made him groan. He couldn't wait to sink his cock to the hilt. To hear her scream as he thrust home. She straightened, lowering her foot to the carpeted floor. If only he had a camera to take a photo of the sexual heaven before him—Allie in nothing but knee-high boots, black lace underwear and thigh-high stockings. *Fuck me.* Her body was built for Playboy, while her face still held sweet seductive charm.

"Take off your panties," he demanded.

She complied, hooking her fingers around the waistband of the tiny strip of material and wiggling until they fell to the floor. With one hand still playing with her pussy, he used the other to fumble with his belt buckle, unclasping it, along with the button on his jeans. He continued moving his fingers inside her, concentrating on the rhythm of her hips, the contraction of her walls.

"Lean over." He lowered his zipper, withholding a groan as she did as requested.

Her ass—holy fuck, her sweet, delicious ass. One day, he'd take her there. She'd whimper, squirm, and moan, but she'd love it. He'd make sure she did. With reluctance, he removed his fingers, trailing them higher, wiping her juices around the tight tempting entrance.

"Mitchell," she warned, flinching at the forbidden touch.

He chuckled. How could one woman be such a mass of contradictions? Over their time together, he'd diminished her inhibitions, made her into a sex kitten who obeyed his every desire...well, all bar one.

"Just teasin', sweetheart." He kicked off his shoes and shucked his jeans, working fast to appease the ache in his groin. He didn't bother removing his shirt and jacket—ain't nobody got time for that—positioned his cock at her entrance and drove home in one spine-tingling thrust.

They moaned in unison while he raked his hand down her spine, enjoying the delicate softness of her smooth skin. She was flawless. Every inch, from her hair to her toes.

"You undo me," he groaned, starting a slow, lazy rhythm. "You always feel so good."

Alana wiggled her ass, encouraging him to take her harder. *Hell no.* He was running this fun house. He continued to move inside her in long strokes, gripping her hips, ending each slide with a grind of his pelvis. She arched her back, her hands clawing at the bed covers, and began rocking faster.

"Slow down, Allie. I don't want to finish this yet."

She whimpered. "Please, Mitchell."

Don't beg me, sweetheart. It drives me wild. She ignored his instruction, moving quicker, making his balls tighten. When the base of his spine began to tingle, he pulled out and pushed her hard onto the bed. She gasped and turned onto her back with a huff.

Another Kodak moment—Allie sprawled on the mattress, legs ajar, pussy on display, breasts thrust high in black lace, with her boots and stockings still on. Hell yeah, he was a lucky son of a bitch.

"You've still got your jacket on." She frowned.

"You've got your boots and stockings on. You don't hear me complainin'."

She glared at him, pulling her legs together. "Take it off. The shirt too."

He raised an eyebrow and contemplated denying her just to increase her feistiness. The softness of her body tempted him too much, and in the end, he shucked his jacket and tugged at the buttons of his shirt until he stood naked before her.

"Better?" he asked, climbing onto the bed and crawling between her toned thighs.

"A little," she snipped, glancing away from him.

It was an act. She'd played hard ball before; however, two could play that game.

"Still not in the mood?" He pulled back, sitting on his haunches.

She shrugged, yet again lying her pretty little ass off. Yet her pussy still glistened with arousal in the dim lighting.

"I'll finish this on my own then, will I?" He grasped the base of his cock and began to stroke, eliciting a moan that made her gaze snap back to his. Fighting laughter, he closed his eyes and continued to taunt her. His touch was light, cautious not to send himself over the edge, yet her image in his mind was enough to make him blow—the boots, the stockings, the cleavage that would bring any man to their knees.

"Fine," she huffed, jostling the bed with her movements. "I'll leave you alone."

He opened his eyes, found her on her hands and knees climbing from the bed, and grabbed her booted ankle, pulling her back. "Don't even think about it." She squealed as he tugged her toward him and flipped her onto her back. "I'm finished playing games, Allie. Spread those gorgeous thighs."

She continued to glare, and he couldn't help smirking at the way she pretended disinterest. She was hot for him, her eyes gleaming with cloying need. He pushed her legs apart and watched her skin break out in goose bumps. She bit her lower lip and stared at him, waiting, wanting more. He gripped her hips, pulled her the final inches toward him, then moved onto his knees to position himself at her entrance.

"You want this fast?" he asked.

"Yeah. I want you to hurry the hell up," she said, with the devil in her eye.

He chuckled and drove into her, leaning over to take her mouth with his. She groaned, met him thrust for hard, unyielding thrust, and parted her lips, allowing his tongue entrance to devour her. They clawed, nipped, ground, fucking like the wild, until sweat began to bead his forehead. He rested on one elbow and pulled down the cups of her bra. His hand worked the soft flesh in his palm, tweaking her nipple between his thumb and forefinger.

"Oh, yes," she panted, rocking harder into him.

His orgasm built with each harsh exhale, with each squeeze of her pussy around his shaft. She was close, too, her eyes wide, her mouth gaping to suck in breath.

"I'm close, Allie. So close."

She swung her legs around his waist. He reached between them to find the small bundle of nerves at the apex of her thighs. As his fingers brushed back and forth over her clit, she gasped, closed her legs tighter around him and bucked.

"Mitchell!"

His name on her lips was his undoing. He thrust hard, the orgasm hitting him with a force that slammed his eyes closed. Rapture took over, rushing from his balls to his cock and into the depths of her sweet heat. She milked him, convulsing around his shaft, drawing out the ecstasy until his body was numb.

He took her mouth, kissing her hard, until her spine relaxed and booted legs fell limp from his waist.

"Oh, god, that was good," she panted.

He hung his head, fighting back a laugh. "I thought you weren't in the mood."

"I thought you had more sense than to taunt me when I'm angry."

Touché. He should shut his mouth while he was ahead. Like every other woman on earth, Allie never forgot a simple argument, let alone the monumental aesthetic issues surrounding Huey, Dewey, and Dickhead.

"Let me run you a hot shower." Yes, he was a suck up, he couldn't help it. Mind blowing sex would do that to a guy.

A LANA WATCHED MITCHELL LEAVE THE ROOM, TAKING HER BLISS WITH HIM. The sex was breathtaking, yet as soon as her body quit convulsing in orgasm, stress showed its sharp claws. With a deep sigh, she pushed from the bed, removed her bra, stockings, and boots, and then shuffled to the bathroom. She leaned against the cold wall, staring at the floor as the shower began to run.

"What's wrong, Allie?"

"Nothing," she replied without thought. She'd been saying the same thing for months. Yet now the situation was worse. There was no way she could pull off the perfect wedding after tonight's events. She couldn't believe her future husband had let the bachelor party get so out of hand. The groomsmen would be the talk of the wedding industry for years to come. And not in a good way.

"The wedding will be fine." Mitch shook water from his arm and stepped toward her.

He didn't understand. He never would. A wedding was different for a woman. It wasn't just an expensive party. Yet for her, making it perfect meant so much more.

"Come on, Allie. It will be." He pulled her into his arms.

She sighed. "Simply saying that doesn't make it so. I still have things to organize, and after what Gabi and Blake are going through, it doesn't seem like the right time."

Mitch pulled back, frowning at her. "You're not thinking of pulling out on me, are you?"

"No." She shook her head. "It's just…"

His eyes widened. "It's just, what?" He gripped her shoulders and stared at her, his dark-brown hair framing hazel eyes.

"Nothing. Forget it." If she tried to explain, he would laugh. The problem was, she didn't want the perfect wedding for herself. She wanted it for him. She wanted to give him something in return for everything he'd given her during their time together.

He narrowed his gaze, and she could still see the taint of liquor in their glassy depths. Hopefully, he wouldn't remember this conversation tomorrow.

"Come on." He took her hand and pulled her under the spray. "I'll get you washed up, and a good night's sleep will fix everything."

She remained quiet while he lathered her body, paying attention to every inch of her skin. When they were both clean, Mitchell turned off the taps and opened the shower door to grab a fresh towel off the rack. "Here."

"Thank you." She stepped from the stall and dried herself before walking from the bathroom, needing space. They'd been together almost twelve months, and in that time, she'd questioned her worth against Mitchell's many times. She wasn't naïve to judge everything based on income, but money, fame, and popularity in comparison to what she had to offer didn't compute well.

The wedding had been her opportunity to introduce herself, and them as a couple, in a professional, yet heartfelt manner. It was her chance to show the guests, most of which she'd never met, that she was worthy of this talented man. And most of all, she wanted to create the perfect atmosphere, to prove to herself, and her future husband, that they were meant to be together.

Now the groomsmen would be the laughing stock of bridal magazines worldwide.

Alana wrapped the towel around herself, securing it above her breasts, and planted herself on the end of the bed. With vivid clarity, she could imagine how the wedding photos would turn out. Laughable. And not in a good way.

"I'll do it all." Mitchell's voice came from the bathroom entry, startling her.

"Excuse me?" She turned, noting the seriousness in his expression. A towel was wrapped around his waist, his hair shaggy and wet, drops of water still falling from the dark strands.

He raised his chin. "Leave the rest of the wedding plans up to me."

"Come again?"

"Didn't we hire a wedding planner for a reason?"

"Yeah but, that defeats the purpose." Alana had wanted to organize it all herself. She'd only hired the planner to do the running around because the streets of New York were still daunting to someone who'd grown up in relative seclusion.

"The purpose is for you to enjoy the day—and the lead up, for that matter. I know every woman wants the fairytale wedding they've dreamed of since childhood—"

"That isn't what I wanted," she blurted, needing to defend herself. It wasn't her dreams she was concerned with. She wanted the start of their lives to run smoothly. Like a good omen. Celebrity marriages had a high failure rate. She didn't need Google to tell her that statistically speaking they were likely to get an early divorce. One magazine had already predicted the month they would split. And although Alana knew their relationship was strong, she still wanted to do everything possible to make it stay that way.

"So what is it, then?"

Alana sighed and focused on the plush pile of the dark pink carpet.

"Allie?"

"It was all for you."

Silence. Mitchell didn't reply, but his gaze heated her skin. When she peered up at him, his stare bore into her, his frown deep. "Explain."

She chuckled in defeat at his gruff order and glanced back to the floor. "The perfect wedding wasn't for me. It was for you. I wanted to create something special, to show you how much I love you, and to give back

94

everything you've given me."

This time when silence filled the room, her heart began to throb. "I want your family and friends to like me. I want them to know that although we come from different lifestyles, we're still meant to be together."

She became restless in the passing seconds, wondering what he was thinking but not daring to lift her gaze.

"Are you for real?" he asked, coming to sit on the bed beside her.

She turned to him. "Yes, Mitchell. I can't shower you in gifts or fly you around the world. You've even paid for almost all of the wedding. All I could do to repay you was to make our special day perfect."

"So all the stress and panic and sleepless nights were for my benefit?"

Alana glanced down at her nails, not wanting to answer. She'd put him through hell the last few weeks with her anxiety tirade, and it wouldn't surprise her if he was a little angry.

"Allie," he laughed, and pulled her into his side. "Your sweetness always surprises me. And now I don't feel so bad about the honeymoon challenge being a fraud."

"Come again?" her gaze snapped to his.

His eyes widened and the smile vanished from his face. "Yeah...about that. The challenges tonight were for your benefit. Leah, Gabi, and I thought it would be nice to give you a crazy night of fun. I never planned on going on an adventure holiday."

"What?" She pushed from the bed and turned on him.

He held up his hands in surrender. "I'm not the one to cast that dirty stare at. It was actually the girls' idea. They wanted to do something wild, came up with the honeymoon challenge, and I honestly didn't think anything bad could come of it."

"Mason's eyebrow, Ryan's tan, Sean's bruised face. You mean to tell me all that could've been avoided?" Alana couldn't believe this. She'd dragged her mom into a strip club, for Christ's sake.

"Well it could've been avoided if you didn't put the beauty salon challenge on the list. But I'm not going to split hairs."

She gaped at him, unsure whether to laugh or cry, be angry or glad. She appreciated the thought, though. Leah, Gabi, and all the guys knew her upbringing had been isolated, yet the execution of the challenges was horrific. She never would've placed things on the list that could get her fiancé arrested if that stupid honeymoon destination hadn't been her motivation.

"Don't go getting angry," he said, pushing from the bed. "We did it for you, just like your Nazi attitude over the wedding was for me."

She gave a defeated laugh and stepped into his waiting arms. She snuggled her head into his neck, and he held her tight, resting his chin in her hair.

"I meant what I said about the wedding. Let me organize whatever is left. I'll work with the planner and make sure things are done properly."

"No, Mitchell. I appreciate the offer, but I still need everything to run smoothly. If not for you, then for my peace of mind." She ran her hands around his waist and clung to him, hoping he would understand. "I want the start of our lives to be perfect—"

"It will be. But it will be perfect for *us*, Allie. Not the guests or the paparazzi. Their happiness and judgments aren't my concern." He kissed her forehead, sending heat through her veins. "As long as the both of us are happy, nothing else matters. And I'm more than capable of organizing that with the wedding planner."

Alana leaned back and raised a brow.

"OK, so maybe I don't have a clue about what's involved. I can figure it out, though. If I need help I'll ask Leah."

"What if—"

"No. No, what if's. Just let me handle it. And if things don't run on schedule or problems arise, that's fine too. You have to draw the line at some point and start making this a day to enjoy, not panic over."

She broke eye contact and sighed. "Yeah, I guess." Anxiety still consumed her, but he would be able to look after the remaining items on her to-do list. She needed to let go of her issues. If Mitchell chose to enlist the help of the wedding planner, it would be a breeze. Alana had wanted to do it all herself, though, making the gift of their special day more meaningful.

"Good." He grinned at her and leaned in for a lingering kiss.

"But," she broke the connection, still confused with the night's events. "I still can't believe the honeymoon challenge was a scam—"

"No more talk about that nightmare. I'm tired, and we have an action-packed week ahead of us."

Alana rolled her eyes. Her man didn't like to argue. There hadn't been many times when he'd made her angry, and when he did, his tactic was either—defuse the situation with sex, or distract, distract, distract.

He took her hand and led her around to the side of the bed, pulling back the rumpled covers. She unwrapped the towel from around her body and handed it to him, before climbing into bed and yanking up the sheet. "I don't get it," she mumbled, wanting to taunt him one last time. "Why would Leah get a clit piercing if she didn't need to?"

Mitchell paused mid stride on his way to the bathroom. "Wait. What?" He turned on his heels, swaying a little as he stared at her with wide eyes.

"Oh, nothing." Alana grinned. "We can talk about it later. Like you said, we have a busy week ahead, and I need to get to sleep."

CHAPTER 14

MITCH STARED OUT THE TINY JET WINDOW, MASSAGING HIS FOREHEAD WITH the tips of his fingers. Alana's tension had transferred to him during the night, and he didn't enjoy the sensation. Tomorrow he was getting married, and he had no idea what the fuck had to be done to achieve that. Why the hell had he offered to take over Alana's responsibilities?

Well, he knew why, he'd been intoxicated and hated seeing his beautiful bride anxious to the point of nausea. But how would having him in the hot seat make things better?

Fucking idiot.

As soon as the plane landed they would check-in to the Waldorf Astoria, and he would sit down with the wedding planner to sort this shit out. The more duties he could palm off to her, the better. Like he explained to Alana last night, only their happiness mattered. He just had to keep reminding himself of that.

"You look nervous," Leah said, looming over his shoulder.

"I *am* nervous," he muttered.

At least, Alana was happy. Since he agreed to handle the last minute disasters, she'd relaxed, and had the first peaceful sleep he'd noticed in the last month. That in itself was a relief. He hadn't realized she'd been close to walking out on the wedding. He was still worried she would leave him standing at the altar, so any problems that did arise would have to be kept between him and the wedding planner.

Once he arrived at the hotel, he would familiarize himself with the Starlight Roof room for the ceremony tomorrow afternoon, and the Grand Ballroom for the reception, and put the final tasks into motion. He'd vowed to take over, and he wouldn't let Alana down...but he had every intention of relying heavily on the wedding planner.

A smile tilted Leah's lips, one that was replaced by teeth biting into her lower lip as she sat down beside him.

"How's your hood?"

She shot him a glare. "Alana told you?"

He smirked, enjoying the blush that tinted his band manager's cheeks. "Yep. Still don't understand why you did it, though. The challenges were for fun. Alana was getting the honeymoon she wanted whether you guys won or not."

Leah groaned. "Tell me about it. All I can say is that champagne and green eyes are my undoing."

Mitch chuckled. "The joys of inebriation. I think Mason and Sean are suffering from the same remorse this morning." He glanced over his shoulder, finding both of them sulking at the back of the cabin. Sean's face was covered in various shades of bruises, while Mason had a Band-Aid covering the area where his eyebrow should be.

"The stupidity of those two will never cease to amaze me. It's my own idiocy that's astonishing."

"Can't you remove the piercing and let it heal?"

"Yeah, but..."

They made eye contact and he noticed her blush hadn't faded. "But?"

She shrugged. "I kinda like it."

He nudged her with his elbow. "You dirty little slut."

She rolled her eyes. "Yeah. *Me* a slut. The woman who hasn't had sex in twelve months because I'm always too busy dealing with the crap you guys pull."

"Ouch. Twelve months?"

She pointed an accusing finger at him. "Do not repeat that."

He held up his hands. "Never. I promise. But Sean would be happy to help you out of the dry spell. All you have to do is ask."

"You forget that I know where he's been." Leah scrunched her nose in disgust. "Well, I probably only know half of where that man has dipped his wick. Even that's enough to turn me off."

"Understandable. Are you back on speaking terms with Ryan yet?"

She shook her head and turned to focus out the window. "He won't talk to me anymore." She let out a deep breath, then glanced back to meet his gaze. "Don't get me wrong, he's civil. He's still a gentleman, holding open doors and using his manners. He'll answer band-related questions whenever I ask." She shrugged. "But the friendship's gone. He can barely look me in the eye."

Ryan and Leah had been close. Because of the group dynamic, they all tended to pair up on tour—Mitch with Blake, Mason with Sean, and because Ryan had been the only married guy for so long, he normally hung out with Leah, while the rest of them seduced groupies. Their disagreement hadn't just been a manager-client tiff, it was the breakup of a close friendship.

"He'll get over it. Once his bruised ego has healed."

"Yeah, I guess so...." She remained quiet for a moment then clapped her hands together as if breaking the spell. "Now, onto a slightly different subject, Alana said you were taking over the wedding plans."

He groaned. "Don't remind me." The thought still made him break out in a cold sweat.

"Do you have any idea of what you're doing?" she raised a brow, her aqua eyes bright and caring.

"No fucking clue. But I've got a plan. If the wedding goes to hell, I'll ply Alana with alcohol until she passes out, then whisper how great the day was until she wakes up the next morning. Sound good?"

Leah shook her head with a chuckle. "Like I said, the stupidity of you guys will never cease to amaze me."

CHAPTER 15

ALANA RELAXED ONTO THE PORTABLE MASSAGE TABLE, TRYING TO ENJOY THE peace that came along with her swanky hotel suite, and the in room spa treatment she'd ordered. The hands of her masseuse rubbed away reality. She breathed through the anxiety, ignoring the need to go in search of Mitchell and interrupt his meeting with Jan, their wedding planner, and concentrated on the strong, skilled hands on her back. And that frame of mind worked until the suite door closed in the distance, and Mitch's footsteps came up beside her.

Letting go of the wedding responsibilities had been as daunting as doing it all herself. But she'd come to terms with a non-perfect wedding. It really didn't matter that guests could be seated next to strangers, and the groomsmen looked like they were students at Clown College. No biggie. And having the threat of her mother doing any number of dramatic things wasn't going to phase her either. Nope. The thought of her mom pulling out a pellet gun, or kicking a male guest in the nuts for saying hello to her was very far from her mind. Absent completely.

The final plans for the wedding must've gone well, though. She hadn't expected Mitchell back from his meeting with Jan for hours.

"I'll take it from here."

Mitchell's graveled tone gave her goose bumps. The warm touch of the masseuse left her skin, replaced with cooler, rougher, more familiar hands.

"No problem, Mr. Davies. I'll come back for my things in a little while."

Soft footfalls drifted into the distance, then the front door squeaked before a faint click when it closed. Each passing second made the tension coil in her belly. She needed to know if the final seating arrangements were in place. If the gifts for the wedding guests had been properly packaged. If the decorations at the reception and ceremony had arrived. The pressure built until she could no longer keep it in. "Is everything sorted for tomorrow?" she blurted, then held her breath, unsure what to expect.

"Everything is fine." His thumbs travelled up either side of her spine, releasing the tension in her muscles. Those hands of his were talented in many ways. It almost made her forget her worries. Almost. "Jan has everything under control."

So he had palmed everything off to their wedding planner. "Is that wise?" She couldn't hide her nervousness. There was barely twenty-four hours until the ceremony started, and these things needed to be organized. "I know it's her job, but we still had to slot a few last minute guests onto tables. I don't want her sitting them in a random place with strangers."

His hands travelled back down her spine, over her waist, then up her sides to brush the swell of her breasts. "I'm going to repeat that everything is under control," he murmured against her ear, "And from now on I will ignore all wedding-related conversations. Let it go and enjoy yourself."

She bit her lip and held in the questions poised on the tip of her tongue. Clearing her mind, she focused on his touch and the way his fingers made her nipples tingle into tight peaks against the warm leather table. "Mmm. That's nice."

"The next twenty-four hours without you is going to kill me." His hands travelled lower, making her core clench as he pushed aside the small towel draped over her ass. Rough fingers gripped the waistband of her silk panties, pulling them down her legs, until she was naked.

"Spare a thought for the woman who has to deal with your soon-to-be mother-in-law."

She heard the slurp of the oil bottle, then his hands were at her ankles, sliding higher to the inside of her thighs until he was poised at her entrance. "Yeah, I don't envy you."

He teased her with his thumb, gliding it over her pussy lips before retreating and running his hands back down to her ankles. He continued to torment her, repeating the movement over and over again until her sex dripped with arousal.

"Mitchell..." She clenched her thighs, trying to alleviate the throb settling between them.

"Yeah, sweetheart?"

"What are you doing?"

He teased her pussy again, this time spreading her lips to glide through her moisture. "I'm giving you a massage," he purred.

Massage my ass. He was slowly killing her. She turned onto her back, resting her legs over either side of the table as she blinked her innocent eyes up at him. "How much would I have to pay to get a full service?"

He cleared his throat, his focus on the apex of her thighs. "I think we can come to a mutually beneficial agreement." He palmed the erection tenting his pants and raised his gaze to her eyes. "After all, this will be my last chance to bed a beautiful woman while I'm single."

She spread her legs wider and crooked a finger for him to join her. Without a word, he removed his shirt, shucked his pants, and climbed onto the slim table between her knees.

He eyed the limited space around her with a frown. "You might need to get on top, baby."

"I can do that." She sat up, slid off the table and waited for him to lie down. Returning the agonizing massage, and teasing him to the point of release would've been enjoyable, but she couldn't wait. Instead, she climbed back onto the table, stabilizing herself on his chest while she straddled his waist.

He palmed his shaft, pressing the tip to her entrance. She closed her eyes, leisurely impaling his cock, savoring every inch. "Oh, god, yes." She moaned, enjoying the way her muscles contracted around him.

Mitchell gripped her hips with one hand while she started to ride him in languorous strokes. "Fuck. You feel good."

She continued to gyrate, increasing the pace, deepening the thrusts. Her clit rubbed against him with each undulation, sending tingling pulses throughout her body. Hitting climax wouldn't take long. She'd denied herself enjoyment for weeks and had a lot of built-up pleasure to release. She could already feel it pooling low in her abdomen.

Mitchell's hand rose to her breast, and she opened her eyes to his hazel stare. His nostrils flared, showing just how close he was to coming as she ground harder. "Come here," he whispered.

She lowered, bringing them chest to chest. His hand moved from her hip, to the back of her head, applying pressure until their mouths were a breath apart. He kissed her hard, his tongue gliding between her lips in hungry need while her pussy continued to contract around him.

"I love you," he murmured.

"I love you, too."

He thrust into her, increasing the pace until the table began to squeak in protest. "I want to watch you come."

He wouldn't have to wait long. She was hovering on the precipice, about to glide over. He continued to meet her undulations, jerking his hips up every time she sank onto him. Their breathing increased, the heavy sounds of sex filling the air, the table creaking louder in disapproval.

Heat built, pleasure heightened, and then she was flying, figuratively, as her climax hit, taking over her body...and literally as the table fractured beneath them. They fell to the floor, Mitchell holding her tight as they landed hard. His hips paused for a second before he continued to rock into her. "Shit," he moaned, pounding with force, coming undone as the final strokes of release assailed her.

Their bodies slowed, she opened her eyes, panting while she surveyed the damage. "I nominate you to explain this to the masseur."

Mitchell's chest vibrated beneath her. "I can picture it now. 'The good news is we're finished with your table. The bad news is we need to buy you a new one.'"

She chuckled, leaning over to wrap her arms around him. Soon he would leave, and she would miss him more with every second. They promised not to talk to one another until they exchanged vows—a commitment she already despised, more so now that the last minute plans were on his shoulders.

"I can hear your thoughts," he whispered into her hair. "And you've got nothing to worry about. Jan has it under control, I've double checked everything, and Leah is on standby in case of emergency."

The thought of a wedding emergency made Alana's skin prickle. She breathed in deep and let out a sigh. "I'm glad." He deserved to know she was excited. And she was. A mix of adrenaline and fear. "All that matters to me now is that I end tomorrow as your wife."

"You will, Allie. And I'll be the envy of every man in the room."

CHAPTER 16

MITCH RELAXED INTO THE FANCY RESTAURANT CHAIR AND SIPPED HIS breakfast coffee. The last thing he needed was caffeine, even after the lousy night's sleep. He'd ordered it to try and pass the time. It was mere hours now. He could probably count it in minutes, but he was too buzzed for that.

"You're not stressing at all, are you?" Blake asked, then shoved a forkful of bacon into his mouth.

"What's to stress about?" A smile widened his cheeks. The organization of the wedding was in the hands of a paid planner and hotel staff, and Alana's anxiety had settled. All he had to do was wait for the big moment.

Blake shrugged. "I don't know. I just thought you'd be peaking out about reciting your vows."

Fuck. Mitch focused over Blake's shoulder, trying to remember the lines he'd memorized weeks ago. They'd totally skipped his mind. *To love and cherish? Shit.* That wasn't one of them.

Blake chuckled. "I guess the deer-in-headlights look means you've reconsidered my question."

"Shut the hell up." *I take you as you are – the woman who stole my heart, and promise to love you for the person you are now, and the one you will grow to be.* "Ha ha ha, sucker." Mitch gave Blake the bird. "I remembered." Well, the start anyway.

"Good for you, buddy." Blake smirked. "I just hope you don't crumple under the pressure of a crowd."

Asshole.

"Mitch!"

They both glanced up at the feminine call to see the wedding planner striding toward them. Her eyes were bright with practiced hospitality as she approached in a tailored skirt suit.

"I'm glad I found you," Jan said with a smile. "I went to your suite. Obviously, you weren't there."

"Obviously," he muttered, still annoyed at having the world's biggest dickwad as his best man. "What's up?"

"Nothing major. I just have a quick question." She pulled up the vacant seat beside him and sat down. "The reception manager called this morning. He wanted to clarify that we hadn't made an oversight on the guest list."

"What oversight?" He ignored the tickle in his chest that warned of impending doom and waited patiently for her answer.

"A Mr. Bowen checked in yesterday afternoon but isn't on the wedding list. I wanted to double-check that we haven't missed him in the seating chart."

"What?" He frowned in confusion. "Mr. & Mrs. Bowen are Allie's grandparents. They were invited to the wedding and should be on the guest list. I remember seeing their names on one of the tables yesterday."

"Yes. Sorry." She smiled in apology. "I mean, this is *another* Bowen. Chris is his name."

Static rang in Mitch's ears, and his heart began to pound at a painful rate. He pushed from his chair, itching for a fight. "What room's he in?"

"He's a wedding guest?" she asked, her gaze moving to Blake for confirmation.

"No. He's not." Mitch ground out. The fucking bastard was far from welcome at their wedding. "Tell me where he is."

Jan's smile faltered as she moved to her feet. "Mitch, I'm sorry, but because you aren't paying for his room, I can't give you that information. I only wanted to confirm if we'd left him off the wedding list."

"No, we haven't left him off the *fuckin'* guest list," he growled, stabbing his fingers through his hair. "He shouldn't be here."

Blake's chair screeched across the floor, and he stood. "Don't get worked up. We'll sort it out. No sweat."

"Give me the room number," he repeated, and a tiny ounce of remorse sunk under his skin at the way Jan jerked back. She didn't reply, just stared at him in shocked silence. He needed to chill. Big breath in. Let it out. He was calm. He was Zen. He wasn't going to freak the fuck out in one of the most pretentious hotels in Manhattan.

"Let me put it this way, Jan," he lowered his voice, not wanting any more unwanted attention from staff or guests. "If Alana finds out he's here, she'll flip. And I'm willing to do everything in my power to stop that from happening." He leaned in close, his gaze almost a glare while he tried to convey his sincerity. "I don't care if I have to knock on every motherfuckin' door in this entire hotel. I will find him, and if I have to, I'll throw him outta here myself. Because jeopardizing my future wife's happiness is my breaking point."

Jan's eyes widened, but he wasn't finished. "I've dealt with her anxiety for weeks. No, months. She's worked hard. She's poured her heart into today, and there's no way I will let her father come in here and fuck that up for her."

"Her father?" Jan repeated on a whisper.

"Yes." He didn't elaborate. Alana's relationship with the man was nobody's business, and Mitch didn't plan on sharing information that could make its way into the tabloids. "So what will it take, Jan? All I need is his room number." He ground his teeth while he waited, every second making his anger more palpable.

"We won't cause any trouble," Blake added, then winced at the lie.

Yeah, getting around this situation without causing trouble wasn't realistic. Mitch already wanted to grab Alana's father around the neck for daring to show up.

"Mitch..." Jan's gaze pleaded as she glanced between them both.

"Come on. We're running out of time." He stepped forward cupping her shoulders. "Please." He raised his eyebrows, begging for the room of the son of a bitch who raped Alana's mother.

"It's on the fifth floor." She sighed. "I'd have to confirm the number."

•••

Mitch strode down the hotel hallway, his eyes skimming the door numbers as he passed. This was the last thing he should be doing on the morning of his wedding.

"Calm the fuck down," Blake ordered. "I can't keep up."

Mitch no longer had hold of his self-control. He was furious that anyone, let alone Alana's father, would dare to ruin their day. And he wouldn't calm down until the asshole who raped his fiancées' mother was as far away as possible. Alana had barely gotten over the whole one-eyebrow, orange tan, and mangled face incident. If she knew Bowen was here, she may not stick around to ask questions.

"I can't," he spoke over his shoulder. "Alana doesn't deserve this. I need to get him out of here. God knows she'll probably take off if anything else goes wrong."

"She wouldn't do that."

Mitch paused and turned on his friend. "No?" He raised a brow. "I wouldn't have thought so either, but you haven't lived with her for the past weeks. She was barely hanging on in Vegas. She puts up with way too much shit to be with me. Us guys are different," he waved between them both. "We have the thrill of performing live, the rush that comes with screaming fans, and a loaded bank account. What does she get? Social media judging her every day. Paparazzi stalking her trips to the store. Seeing her father will spook her, and I won't risk her running out on me."

"She isn't going to run," Blake muttered. "You're both nervous, that's all."

Mitch ground his teeth in frustration. Blake didn't get it. He had no fucking clue. Gabi was a strong willed woman of the world. Although Alana was growing into a capable and highly-independent woman, she was still vulnerable, in need of his protection. But arguing the point was useless, and Mitch didn't have time to waste.

He turned and didn't stop his angered footfalls until he reached Chris Bowen's door. Moments later, Blake was at his side, and they both knocked on the heavy wood in unison.

"Just remember to keep your cool," Blake said, "If you pop the old-timer again, you'll probably end up in the slammer."

What cool?

Mitch heard the door chain release, then there was a heartbeat of silence. Alana's father must be looking through the peep hole, weighing up his options. Then the large wooden door opened a crack, and the familiar face stared back at him.

"Mitchell," the man said in greeting.

"You need to leave." *Common courtesy, kiss my ass.*

Chris shook his head. "I'm sorry. That's not going to happen." He went to close the door and Blake put his foot in the jam, pushing the door wider with a heavy palm.

"I don't think you heard him," Blake growled. "Pack your shit and get out. Now."

"Or what?" Alana's father turned his gaze from Blake, back to Mitch. They stared at one another, the older man appearing tired and weary, while Mitch fought not to sneer. "You going to hit me again, son?"

"I'm not your fucking son," Mitch snapped.

"No?" He raised a questioning brow. "Just soon to be my son-in-law."

"You're blood might flow through her veins, but you aren't her father."

"She will always be my daughter," Chris said in defeat. "She's always been a part of my life, even though I've never been a part of hers."

The retort clenched at Mitch's heart. Alana was an amazing woman who deserved the love of a doting father. Yet, no matter how much this man cared about her, or wanted to mend the bridges of the past, today, or tomorrow, was not the time to start.

"I won't let you hurt her."

"All I want is to see my daughter on her wedding day."

"All I want is a fluffy pink unicorn," Blake drawled, "But that ain't gonna happen."

Mitch filled his lungs with a deep breath, pictured his future wife in his mind and commanded himself to calm the fuck down. "Seeing you without warning will devastate her. Do you want that?" He raised a taunting brow. "Are you that selfish?"

"She doesn't need to see me. I don't want to make a scene. All I want is a glimpse of her on the most important day of her life. Is that too much to ask?"

"Yeah, it is," Blake replied. "Get tomorrow's newspaper, I'm sure they'll have photos."

"Look." Chris opened the door wider. "I stood back and allowed Alana's mother to raise my daughter without me. I've paid for my mistakes since the day she was born. I'm not doing it anymore."

Mitch glared at the man and shook his head. His fury grew, making his hands shake and his heart palpitate. Unless he wanted to physically remove the guy from the building—which legally he'd have no right to do—Mitch had to come up with a different strategy.

"Fine." He raised his chin and fisted his hand. "Just realize that if you show up to the wedding, I'll make sure you regret it."

"I'm a lawyer, son. I know where I can and cannot be."

Son. Mitch's eye twitched, and he was glad Blake took over, looming forward, laughing with derision.

"Yeah," Blake replied in a deathly tone. "And I'm the motherfucker who doesn't give a shit about your rights. You mess with my friends, and I'll make you my bitch." He stepped back, staring Chris down. "Have a lovely afternoon, Mr. Bowen."

CHAPTER 17

M ITCH SAT ON ONE OF THE GUEST CHAIRS IN THE SILENT GRAND BALLROOM, massaging his forehead to relieve his headache. The room was a mass of glittering lights, polished silver, and heavily scented flowers. It was beautiful, sweet, and reminded him of his future wife. She'd done an outstanding job pulling a celebration this size together, especially when she'd never attended a wedding before.

"How long is she going to be?" Mason broke the silence. He leaned against the back of a chair on the next table, staring at Mitch with concern. They all did—Blake, Ryan, Sean.

"She said she was on her way," Blake murmured.

They were waiting for Jan. The miraculous wedding planner who Blake tried to convince him would fix everything.

"I can't sit here doing nothing for much longer," Mitch muttered. He was going to be late. Not that he had much to do, but the stylist had already been in his suite for over half an hour.

Minutes of tension-filled silence continued, before the sound of a door opened and feminine heels clicked on the floor. "Sorry I'm late," Jan said, striding toward them. "It took a while to pull everything together."

"And?" Mitch asked, shifting forward to sit on the edge of his seat.

"You've got nothing to worry about," she replied, coming to stand beside him. "I've doubled the security team. There will be men scattered everywhere. Alana's father won't get anywhere near her."

Mitch scrutinized the wedding planner's confidence.

"I know what I'm doing." She gave him a half-hearted smile. "We've also increased security in the elevators so only staff members with a security card can escort guests to the venue floors. The added guards are merely for your own peace of mind."

Mitch nodded, the slight sense of relief loosening the vice grip on his lungs. He scanned the faces of his friends, reassured with their looks of approval.

"Sounds good," Blake spoke up. "He can't get to the wedding via the elevators, and security can make sure he doesn't come in through the staircase."

"Can't you just kick him out?" Mason asked in annoyance. "I'm sure Mitch has spent enough money here to earn him that privilege."

Jan sighed. "Mr. Bowen is a hotel guest, and at the moment he hasn't done anything wrong. And besides that, removing him will create a scene with the paparazzi. We already have a crowd at the front doors, and any public spectacle has the possibility to get back to Alana before the wedding." Jan's eyes turned grim. "I can't stop you from taking matters into your own hands, but for the sake of your happiness, I think you should leave it alone. Let security do their job and try to forget about him."

Mitch released a bark of laughter. "Yeah, I'll try and do that."

"I'm sorry this has happened." Jan winced. "I'll do everything in my power to make the day go smoothly."

"I still think breaking the guy's legs would be the best option," Sean announced.

"Then we'd get incarcerated before the wedding even starts," Mason argued. "And I'd end up being someone's bitch because I'm better looking than all of you."

Blake rolled his eyes, and Ryan shook his head.

Sean elbowed Mason in the ribs. "Well, you are the biggest pussy."

Jan cleared her throat and ignored the commentary. "Honestly, I've got enough security to guard a royal wedding. Her father won't get anywhere near her."

Mitch ignored the thumping of his heart and nodded. There was nothing else he could do. "Fine." He turned his attention to the groomsmen. Blake in particular. "I don't want any of the girls knowing about this." Asking his best friend to keep this from his wife was rough, but it was the only way to ensure Alana didn't get upset before the ceremony.

Blake nodded.

"She won't find out," Ryan murmured. "We'll make sure of it."

"OK then." Mitch pushed from the chair. "Let's get this show on the road."

•••

Alana stood in front of the full-length mirror, trying to ignore the way her throat tightened in excitement. The reflection before her made her lips tremble. The ivory dress clung to her waist, the skirt billowing out in a mass of gorgeous waves, while the beaded crystals of the bodice glinted in the light. And with the professional make-up and hairstyle, she barely recognized herself. Yet for the first time in a long while, she felt relieved.

She'd awoken this morning with a clear mind and a smile on her face, ready and more than eager to stride down the aisle and marry the man of her dreams. Her previous anxiety had vanished, replaced with a nervous anticipation that tickled her stomach. For weeks, she'd stressed that there wasn't enough time to get everything done. Now she wished the minutes would pass quicker, instead of the torturously slow tick, tick, tick of the clock.

Her mom's sniff broke the silence and Alana turned, dragging the heavy material of her skirt around to face the only other person in the main bedroom.

"I've never seen anything so beautiful." Her mom inhaled a ragged breath and lifted a white handkerchief to her nose. "I haven't told you lately, or enough throughout your life. But I'm so proud of the woman you've become."

"Thank you," Alana whispered. The words brought tears to her eyes. They'd never been an openly emotional family, and praise hadn't been easy to earn. Her mom held out her hands, and Alana took them, enjoying the familiar comfort of her touch.

"I've been the child in our relationship for a long time," her mother uttered softly. "You're wise beyond your years, and I've always been a challenge."

"If I cry, my make-up will be ruined."

Her mother chuckled and squeezed Alana's hands. "I know. I know." She shook her head. "I wasn't going to say anything. But you deserve to hear how I feel. Mitch is a nice guy, and although no man will ever be worthy of you, I think the two of you make a great couple."

Dealing with the changes in Alana's life had been hard for a mother who couldn't stand the company of men. There had never been a kind word spoken about the lead guitarist, no praise, no affection. Yet Alana had always known it was there...somewhere.

"Mitchell is a great man," she replied.

Her mom sighed with a nod. "Yes, he is. And if he ever hurts you, I'll rip his balls off."

Any other daughter would've laughed. Alana couldn't. Her mother was dead serious. "OK," she said with hesitation. "Good to know." She leaned in, gently hugging her mom so they didn't crumple or smudge anything.

"I love you, sweetheart." The words murmured past Alana's cheek.

"I love you, too."

For most of Alana's life, it had been the two of them. Yes, the retreat she grew up on had housed many women. But they came and went, never sticking around for more than a year or two. This lady had been the only constant throughout her life until she found Mitchell.

"I'm proud of you, too," Alana added. "Being here is hard for you."

"You don't need to worry about me."

Alana did, though. Her grandparents had been unable to attend the engagement party, so today would be the first time her mother came face to face with the parents of the man who raped her since before Alana was born.

"Your grandparents are lovely people," she continued. "I spent half my childhood in their house. It will be...nice to catch up with them again."

Alana pulled back and raised a brow.

"OK, that could be the shrink talking." Her mom grinned. "But I can't wait to see my baby girl walk down the aisle. I wouldn't miss it for the world."

Silence hung heavy between them, clutching at Alana's heart.

"Your father was a great man once. Well, a boy, really."

Alana froze. They never spoke about Chris Bowen. Ever. And even though the need to find out more about him clawed at her every day, she hadn't been able to bring herself to discuss it with her mom. She'd already been through enough. That's why Alana had become close to her grandparents. Mr. and Mrs. Bowen answered the questions she couldn't ask her mother.

"I loved him."

Alana nodded, wrinkling her nose to dissuade the tingling sensation. From what her grandparents had told her, her mom and Chris had been high school sweethearts. Inseparable. Until the night Alana was conceived.

A knock sounded at the door, breaking the moment, and Gabi popped her head inside. "The photographer—" Gabi's mouth widened, and she pushed the door open, stepping into the room. "Oh, Alana."

Her maid of honor strode forward in a crimson bridesmaid gown, her eyes wide, her hair pinned back in curls. "You look so pretty."

"We're running out of time, ladies." The photographer stepped into the room and paused. "Whoa. You make a stunning bride."

Butterflies exploded in Alana's belly. All that stood between her and the wedding ceremony was the photographs that needed to be taken. Twenty minutes of smiles and laughter, then she'd be beside Mitchell.

"I'm nervous," she admitted, then blinked in shock at the first burst of bright camera flash.

The photographer grinned. "That smile is too cute to miss."

Hundreds of snaps later, the photographer left with the promise of a thousand more to come.

"We're late," Alana squeaked.

Leah grabbed Alana's arms, stopping her from scurrying like a mad woman. "You're meant to be late. That's one of the bride's duties."

"Take a deep breath," Gabi added, rubbing the tense muscles between

116

Alana's shoulder blades. "Have you got everything you need? Flowers? Perfume? Lipstick?"

Kate stepped forward. "It's all here." She held up Alana's bouquet of red roses in one hand and her white clutch in the other.

"Are you able to look after my bag until the reception?" Alana turned to her mom in panic.

"Relax, sweetheart. I can take care of anything you need."

Alana sucked in a breath. Right now all their guests would be seated in the Starlight Roof room. Her fiancé would be joking with his groomsmen, nervous, and hopefully excited. And her grandfather would be standing near the entry to the ceremony, ready to escort her down the aisle.

"Do you want a drink to ease your nerves?" Leah asked.

"No!" *God, no.* Anything that reached her stomach would make a second appearance during the wedding vows.

"Let's go, then." Her mother's words were soft, slow, deliberately calm. Not that it helped.

Alana grabbed for her bouquet, thankful to have something to cling to, and followed Gabi to the suite door. With each step her heart thumped harder, threatening to explode.

"This is it," Gabi spoke, her grief masked behind an enthusiastic smile.

Alana stared at the heavy wood of the door, the image of Mitchell taking over her mind. She couldn't wait to be with him, to see his reaction, and hear the first words that left his lips. Her focus was consumed with him. Then Gabi opened the door, and two men stood before her. Two large, broad chested men in tailored suits.

"Hello, Ms. Shelton. It would be our honor to escort you to your wedding today."

CHAPTER 18

ALANA STARED AT THE TOWERING MEN. "WHO ARE YOU?"

"Hotel security, ma'am. Your husband decided to take a few last minute precautions to ensure your perfect day runs smoothly."

Alana glanced over her shoulder and frowned at her mother. "Did you know about this?"

"No." She shook her head. "I'm sure everything's fine."

A tightening in Alana's stomach told her otherwise. Mitchell wasn't the precautionary type. He tended to fly by the seat of his pants, sorting or skimming over problems as they occurred.

She turned back to the guards and stepped into the hall. "Was there a reason for the heightened security?"

The men exchanged glances, silently answering her question.

"*What* happened?" She breathed deep, trying not to let anxiety take hold. "Is Mitchell all right?"

"I promise it's nothing to worry about." One of the men smiled, extending his arm toward the elevator. "Just an extra precaution due to the crowd outside."

She stood still, unconvinced, with the pressure behind her sternum building. Her emotions were already on overdrive, and her nerves had been frayed for weeks.

"Stop worrying." Gabi grabbed the crook of Alana's arm and led her down the hall. "It's too late to panic now, you're about to get married."

Married. The tightness under her ribs eased, replaced with a burst of adrenaline that shot to her fingertips. All the plans were finalized, and the guests would be seated. Finally, it was time.

"Just picture Mitch. I bet he's freaking out, wondering if you're coming."

"Yeah, I know." Alana checked to make sure her mother, Leah, and Kate were walking behind her. Then she followed the men to the elevator. She fiddled with the beads on her bodice, smoothed the ribbon surrounding her rose stems, and listened to the static ringing in her ears until the ding of the elevator startled her.

"You're fine to go inside Ms. Shelton." One of the guards held open the doors while the other ambled in, situating himself behind a younger man at the button panel.

They even had staff manning the elevators?

"Are you sure?" She raised a brow. "I don't want to get in there if a ninja is likely to fall from the roof." The guard inside the elevator raised his gaze upward, and she didn't know if she should laugh or cry. "What the hell is going on?"

"Come on, Alana. We can't keep the bad influence you call your fiancé waiting."

For once her mother's taunt slid off her back. Something serious had happened to cause the extra security.

"Ma'am?"

The guard holding the door focused on her in concern, yet his voice didn't penetrate. Her blood began to pound while her mind strolled down a nightmarish path. What was happening upstairs? Had one of Mitchell's ex-girlfriends showed up? Did the paparazzi make it into the hotel? Or had someone been hurt by an extremist trying to gain media attention?

Oh, god, control yourself.

She shook her head, dislodging the insanity. It was nerves. That was all. The sleepless nights, and fear of not living up to expectations had gotten to her. And she finally had to let it go.

"Let's do this." She took a deep breath and stepped into the elevator.

Nobody else mattered. No one but the man of her dreams who would be impatiently waiting for her to arrive.

•••

Mitch stood, nervous as shit, before a crowd of family, friends, and music colleagues. He smiled the best he could, jerked his head in greeting at people he hadn't seen in months, and clutched at the tissues in his pockets to wipe the sweat from his palms. He couldn't even make eye contact with his mother in the front row. The nervousness in her gaze made his heart beat louder.

Alana was already fifteen minutes late. He'd expected this, had anticipated the tension filling his body, yet nothing prepared him for the blood-chilling fear that she might not turn up.

"I tell ya, she's not comin'," Mason drawled. The arrogant fucker had his thumbs in his pockets, rocking back and forth on his heels as he smiled at the ladies in the crowd.

"Shut your trap," Blake muttered.

"What?" Mason chuckled, looking at Mitch. "Do you really think she's not going to show up? Christ, man. Wake up to yourself. You two are so full of that lovey dovey shit that it makes me want to shove forks in my eyes."

"How the hell do you pick up women?" Ryan asked, incredulous. "You're such an asshole."

"Treat 'em mean, keep 'em keen, buddy." Mason shrugged. "And it helps that I'm fucking awesome."

"Not so fucking awesome with one eyebrow," Mitch bit back, receiving a filthy glare in return.

"The make-up artist said the drawn on one looks exactly the same as the one you robbed from me."

Sean choked on a laugh. "Bro, the make-up artist lied."

The groomsmen didn't scrub up too bad. Sean was smothered in foundation to cover his bruising. Mason's drawn on eyebrow would appear more believable once they were all drunk. And Ryan had spent hours in the shower with a scourer, lessening the shade of his orange skin.

"And you think I'm the fucking asshole," Mason muttered, turning his back to the crowd.

The celebrant cleared his throat, and they all turned to the front of the room, smiling with apology at the elderly man. *Come on, Allie. Please, hurry up.*

Mitch was worried her father had caught up with her. The guy was a lawyer, he could talk his way into any situation. Then the aftermath would be brutal, not only for Alana, but her mother too. The wedding would be a nightmare, and he couldn't stand the thought of that happening to the sweet woman who made his life complete.

The morning had been tainted with worry. His friends tried to keep him occupied, diverting his attention. And even though Mason liked to focus his remarks on the probability that Alana wasn't going to show, he still appreciated the assholes' efforts. They were there for him, and were also there for his future wife.

"Go time," Blake murmured, turning back to face the guests.

Wait. What? The tinkling sound of a harp flittered through the room, and Mitch snapped his gaze toward the musicians waiting in the back corner. Jan was beside them, folder clutched to her chest as she smiled brightly at him.

Holy shit, it was happening.

Alana was here. They were about to get married. And suddenly it became harder to breathe.

"It's time, buddy," Blake said, patting him on the back. "Now, try not to fuck this up."

CHAPTER 10

ALANA GLANCED AT THE FLOOR, NERVOUSNESS BLINDING HER VISION, MAKING everything blur. Her grandfather stood beside her, his frail arm around her shoulders.

"Are you ready, child?"

Her heart kicked up a gear—if that were even possible—and she breathed deeply as she nodded. She could feel the comforting stares of Leah and Kate, their encouraging words not even registering over the buzz in her ears.

In less than half an hour, with a few graceful steps and whispered vows of love, her life would change. She would no longer be single and alone. She would be the wife of a rock star, his symbol of everlasting love encircling her ring finger, and his commitment forever tattooed on her heart.

She just needed to take that first step.

The high delicate notes of a harp broke the sound of chatter from the church pews in the next room, and the sweet feminine voice that followed stole her breath. She knew this song. When Mitchell asked to take care of the music for the wedding, she hadn't known what to expect. But this acoustic rendition of Bryan Adams' "Heaven" was so perfect it brought tears to her eyes.

"Don't cry," her grandfather whispered, squeezing her tighter. "The man you love is waiting in the next room. I'm sure you don't want him to see you with smeared make-up."

Alana pressed her lips together and admired the elderly face of the only father figure she knew. They hadn't known each other long, yet their bond had been immediate and unbreakable. Without him, she'd be in a tangled mess of bridal material and used tissues. She blinked away the moisture in her eyes, wordlessly nodding again. Her throat was too dry to speak, and even if she did, the broken words would crumple her resolve.

Leah glanced over her shoulder from her position at the front of the bridesmaids. "Next time we talk, you'll be a married woman." She raised her bouquet of lilies and winked as she disappeared into the Starlight Roof room.

"Oh, g-god." Alana choked.

"You'll be fine," Kate assured her. "Smile, raise your chin, and take a deep breath. It'll be over before you know it, so enjoy every second." She straightened her shoulders and followed after Leah.

"Now it's my turn." Gabi grinned. "You know what I'm going to say right?"

Alana shook her head. She had no clue, and lacked the brain capacity to contemplate. All she wanted to know was how she was going to make her numb legs get down the length of the aisle.

"You're marrying Mitchell Davies. *The* Mitchell Davies. Can you believe it?"

Alana shook her head again, the numbness from her legs moving up to consume the rest of her body.

"You're one lucky lady, Alana. And I'm so happy for you." Gabi leaned in, placing an air kiss near her cheek. "I don't want to ruin your face. You look so pretty."

A chuckle bubbled from Alana's belly. "Go," she croaked. "Otherwise Mitchell will start to worry that I'm not coming."

"All right. All right. Watch me work my magic." Gabi turned her back to Alana, wiggled her ass, then started forward.

Alana paused, letting the romantic lyrics sink into her heart before she inhaled a deep steadying breath. "OK," she whispered, squeezing the crook of her grandfather's elbow in one hand while the other held her bouquet high and steady. "It's time to get married."

They shuffled to the open entryway, the heavy swish of her skirt fabric sounding around them. She lowered her gaze, unable to look ahead. She didn't know how her body would react at the sight of Mitchell. Maybe she would freeze. Maybe she would pass out. Either way she didn't want to risk it. Instead she focused on the dark red carpet lining the aisle—the plush pile, the stitching around the border, and took the first step.

Soft voices whispered past her ears, murmurs from celebrity guests and influential people in the music industry. They were all here, their focus trained on her movements. Their attention made her skin clammy. She wasn't used to being in the spotlight. Ever. Her life had been seclusion and loneliness...until she met Mitchell.

Another step.

The final chorus started, building in volume and emotion. Alana felt it in her veins, heating her blood, the lyrics becoming a part of her love for Mitchell. She couldn't avert her gaze any longer. She needed to see his smile, and fall into the depths of his hazel irises.

Gradually, she raised her stare—to the people in the pews she passed, the finely carved stone archways, and finally to the man of her dreams. He stood tall before her, his grin wide, his eyes gleaming.

"Stop," she whispered and her grandfather obeyed, stiffening beside her. She ignored the panic in his posture and took a moment for herself, capturing the fantasy before her, memorizing it for the rest of her life. "I'm blessed."

Mitchell looked proud and refined. His gorgeous groomsmen at his side. Her mother stared back at her from the first pew, and Alana smiled back.

"Yes, child, but your future husband is starting to panic, so consider continuing down the aisle for his sake."

Alana glanced back at Mitchell, and a pang of regret clenched her stomach. His forehead was now creased with concern, his lips held in a tight line.

"OK." Heat entered her cheeks. She hadn't meant to cause alarm, she just wanted to capture the perfection. And she had. It was in her heart, filling her chest to capacity, and no matter what the future handed them, she would always have this moment in time to remember.

•••

Mitch's legs were about to give out. His over-priced suit was making him sweat, his hands were shaking, but no matter how nervous he became, he didn't want to wipe the cheesy-ass grin from his face. Alana stole his breath. His words. His thoughts. She was exquisite in her sparkling white dress, her hair in loose waves around her shoulders.

Heaven. The song he picked couldn't have been more suitable. He was already there, in paradise, with the one person in the world who understood him. Soon his ring would be on her finger, and he would be permanently attached to the most beautiful woman he'd ever known—inside and out. She was his soul mate. The one who made even the worst of days brighter...but he needed to take a piss. And holy shit, he'd forgotten his vows.

He glanced at his groomsmen in panic, the blood draining from his face.

"You look a little pasty, bro." Blake smirked.

"I can't remember what I'm meant to do."

Mason leaned over Blake's shoulder. "It's easy. All you have to do is hand over your balls and spend the rest of your life in misery."

Mitch shook his head, laughter bubbling from his chest as he placed a palm over Mason's face and pushed him back in line. The four men to his right were assholes. The biggest assholes he'd ever met. Yet they were the best men he would ever be lucky enough to call friends, too.

Who cared if he forgot what to say? They'd figure it out together, his groomsmen, the bridesmaids, and his future wife. It may not feel like it to anyone else, but to him, they were all in this together. They were family.

Alana stopped before him, her green eyes wide and hypnotizing. For a moment, he contemplated halting the ceremony, taking her back to the suite and stripping the material from her slowly, lavishing every inch of skin he exposed. Then his dick gained interest, and the last thing he wanted was an erection in front of a room packed full of people.

Getting the formalities out of the way, he shook her grandfather's hand, thanked him for escorting his breathtaking bride, and then turned to the woman in question. "You're..." he wriggled his nose, relieving some of the tingling in his eyes. He'd said it once, and he'd say it again, he was a lucky son of a bitch.

"Smokin'," Mason interrupted, increasing her dazzling smile.

"Hot, Allie," Sean added.

Ryan leaned forward from the end of the line. "Beautiful."

"Yeah, Al," from Blake. "You don't look too bad, honey."

Her eyes glittered brighter with each compliment until the shimmer of tears marred their depths.

"Don't cry." Mitch swiped the hair back from her shoulders, allowing her diamond necklace to sparkle in the afternoon sunlight streaming through the floor to ceiling windows. "You take my breath away."

She lowered her gaze, the dimples at the side of her smile becoming deeper as her cheeks darkened. "Thank you," she whispered, peeking up underneath dark lashes. "Is everything OK? The extra security detail made me worry."

His gaze flashed to the guards in the back corners of the room. They didn't draw attention, but they were still there, hovering unnecessarily. He took her hand, clutching it tight until it stopped shuddering beneath his. "Just a precaution, sweetheart. Everything is fine." He wouldn't elaborate on why he needed to make the security changes. That conversation would come later, hopefully once the night ended without drama.

She nodded, squeezing his fingers, her face alight with excitement.

"Are you ready?" he asked, eager to get started, to claim her for eternity.

"Yes." She straightened her shoulders and bit her bottom lip. "Let's do this."

CHAPTER 20

ALANA NUZZLED INTO MITCH'S NECK, THE WARMTH OF HER BREATH HEATING his sensitive skin. They danced in a slow swaying rhythm, the stress of the ceremony and reception speeches finally over as Mason sang and Ryan played the guitar to an acoustic version of "Unchained Melody" by the Righteous Brothers.

"I love this song," she whispered, kissing the sweet spot below his ear.

"I know." He held her tighter, one arm around her waist, with his free hand tangled into the hair at her nape. He knew the music she loved and prepared the night's playlist to focus on that. Mason and Ryan would do acoustic versions of the slow songs, while another band got the guests on their feet for high-energy dancing.

"Who would've known you were such a romantic man?" she teased, pulling back to meet his gaze.

"Only for you, Mrs. Davies." God, he loved the sound of that. She was his, for now and always, and heaven help anyone who tried to tear them apart. He inclined his head, brushing his lips against hers, and delighted in the way she sank into his chest. Her arms moved over his shoulders, around his neck, and they stared longingly at one another in silence.

"I'm sorry to interrupt," a feminine voice spoke beside him.

Alana pulled back, and he groaned at the break in their heated connection.

"Everything all right, Jan?" he muttered, his focus never wavering from the beauty in his arms. The wedding planner's work for the night was over, everything had been a success, guests were starting to leave, and he planned on getting lucky in less than twenty minutes—five if his dick got its way.

"Alana, can I speak to your adoring husband for a second?"

Mitch glanced at Jan, his senses now on alert as he noted the way she nervously flicked her fingers over a small envelope in her hand.

"OK." Alana stepped from his embrace.

"Finally," Ryan huffed from beside them. "I was wondering when I'd get my turn to dance with the bride." He grabbed hold of Alana's hand and spun her into his arms.

Mitch let out a relieved breath. He had a sense he didn't want his bride near that envelope and was thankful for Ryan's distraction. "Just keep your hands above the waist, brother."

"I'll be a perfect gentleman." Ryan winked, then pivoted on his toes, spinning Alana around the dance floor until her laughter rose over the music.

Mitch chuckled. He didn't have to worry about Ryan's hands. The guy effortlessly won the hearts of ladies simply for being a smooth mother-fucker. Not that it mattered. The rhythm guitarist had never strayed from his wife, and Mitch didn't think he ever would.

As the two of them danced into the crowd, he turned to Jan, the humor vanishing from his system. "What is it?"

"Follow me." She led him behind the deserted bridal table, and held up the envelope. "It's a letter from Alana's father. He left it at the reception desk and asked that it be given to her."

Son of a bitch. "Are you kidding me?" Mitch had only begun to relax from the threat of Chris Bowen in the last hour. Couldn't the man have waited until tomorrow? Didn't he realize how much this would destroy his daughter's night?

Jan shook her head. "I'm giving it to you to do what is best for your wife. I don't want to ruin her wedding day, only I have no business keeping this from you."

Mitch clenched his jaw and took the letter. "Do you know what's inside?" It could be a note, or a gift. Either way he didn't want to give it to Alana, but he felt the same guilt as Jan. He no longer had a legitimate reason to keep this a secret.

"Sorry. I have no clue. I do know he's still in the hotel, though."

He nodded, staring at the black script of Alana's name on the front. "Thank you. I'll deal with it."

"Again, I'm sorry." She squeezed his upper arm, conveying her sincerity with pained eyes. "I wish you all the best for the remainder of the night."

•••

Ryan held Alana close, enjoying the proximity of a feminine body a little too much. Not in a sexual way. Christ, no. He missed the way a lady could soothe his darkest thoughts with the graze of her hand or a simple hug.

In the past months, he'd lost the two most important women in his life, and the void was agonizing. His wife, the one he vowed to spend the rest of his life with, couldn't even attend the wedding of one of his closest friends. That kick in the balls still stung. She hadn't felt "up to it." Hell. For Ryan, it was the final straw on top of a ten-story haystack.

Then there was Leah. The woman he'd considered his best friend. The shock of her betrayal still tortured him. He never would've imagined she would hide something from him, especially a monumental rumor revolving around his marriage to Julie.

"I wonder what that's about," Alana murmured, breaking the spell of his self-pity. She was perched on her tippy toes, peering over his shoulder at Mitch and the wedding planner.

Ryan pulled her close, spinning her until she squealed. Mitch had worked hard to keep family drama away from his bride today. The least Ryan could do was keep her occupied while the groom dealt with whatever had upset Jan. "I'm sure it's nothing."

"He's not happy."

Ryan pivoted on his toes, turning Alana so her back faced her husband. No, his friend didn't look happy. In the brief moments Ryan watched the two speak, Mitch's features changed from confusion, to annoyance, to barely contained anger.

Worst thing was, Ryan was envious of Alana's concern. When was the last time his wife had given a fuck about him? Two years? Three? Even the physical act of making love had left them long ago, and now he was suffering from the worst case of blue balls in history.

"I think I better check on him." Her hands fell from his neck.

"No." He grabbed her hand and pulled her tighter into his body. "This is my dance." He spun her again, keeping his focus away from her curious stare while he dragged her to the far end of the dance floor.

"Ryan?"

"Hmm?" He continued to divert his gaze. Alana wasn't stupid, she'd soon work out that something important was happening, and had been all day. He only needed to keep her occupied for a little longer.

"What's going on?"

He shrugged, trying to conjure a plan, yet the free scotch he'd been drinking made that difficult. "I was hoping you wouldn't notice." Notice what, he had no clue, but keeping her here and talking was the only thing he could come up with.

She paused, waiting for him to continue.

He glanced over his shoulder, found Mitch still chatting with Jan and decided to have a little fun. "OK. Fine." He huffed. "I'm finding it a challenge to keep the commander in line." He released a hand from her waist and subtly pointed to his crotch.

Her mouth widened as her gaze lowered between them, then back up again. When she made eye contact, he pressed his lips together, trying not to chuckle at the horror in her features.

"Ryan! What the hell has gotten into you?" She playfully slapped at his chest and made a move to walk away.

He laughed—the first real, freeing laugh he'd experienced in a long time. He'd turned into a quiet, well-mannered gentleman when he married Julie. It was a hard switch from the partying teenager he'd been, yet he willingly changed his ways out of respect for his wife. Now, each day that passed made him yearn for the wildness the rest of the Reckless guys had been living for years. He missed flirting. He missed fun. Most of all he missed his wife, but he didn't think he would ever get that woman back. Not the caring woman he'd married, anyway.

In two quick steps, he caught up to Alana and grabbed her hand, pulling her back. "Come on, Allie, I was joking. You do look gorgeous, though, and the big man notices these things."

She placed her hands on his chest to stable herself. "Wow. Where did this flirtatious, rock star stereotype come from, Ryan Bennett? I was beginning to think you didn't have a mischievous bone in your body."

"Oh, I've gotta bone all right."

Alana snorted, drawing the attention of couples dancing close by.

"OK. So maybe I took it a little too far." He shrugged.

"Yeah. Maybe." Alana nodded and they both laughed together, only this time his laughter died out in anguish.

He wanted what Mitch and Alana had. *Fuck.* Even with the sorrow Gabi and Blake were going through, he would much prefer to suffer in the arms of a loved one, than ache over the slow agony of a dying relationship.

"You OK?"

He clenched his jaw and swallowed over the dryness in his throat. "Yeah." He had to do something about his marriage. Make a decision. Was he in or out?

"I hope Julie feels better soon."

His nostrils flared as he stared into Alana's eyes. He took her pity head on, because apparently now he was a masochistic motherfucker. "We both know she's not sick."

Alana winced. "I'm sorry, Ryan. Have you patched things up with Leah yet?"

He sucked in a breath. He wasn't doing this tonight. The place for this shit was on Dr. Phil, not the dance floor of his friend's wedding. "I'm not going there." He couldn't, because he still refused to admit that the broken friendship with his band manager hurt more than the shit going down with Julie.

"I understand."

No, she didn't. Nobody did. Until a few days ago, he'd been the only married member of the group. None of them knew what long-term commitment was. They didn't understand the strain that festered when you left your wife home alone for weeks on end, while you toured the globe.

"Do you want me to take you back to Mitch?" He asked, having enough of the deep and meaningful game. He tried to keep her occupied for as long as possible, but now he needed booze. Hard, numbing booze.

He glanced around the ballroom, finding the groom a few feet away, watching them. Ryan jerked his head, telling Mitch to come fetch his woman. "I'll leave you both to it."

"Thank you for the dance." Alana leaned in, placed a gentle kiss on the stubble at his cheek and turned to her husband. "Is everything all right?"

Ryan paused, hovering for a moment to see if everything was all right.

"No, Allie. I'm sorry. We need to talk."

ALANA FOCUSED ON THE ENVELOPE MITCHELL TAPPED AGAINST HIS SUIT-CLAD chest. It was plain, white, with the hotel insignia on the front, along with her name.

"It's a letter." He held it out to her. "From your father."

Her gaze shot to his. "I don't understand." She took the envelope and fingered the crisp edges. Her throat tightened, and nausea grew low in her belly. "Why is my father sending me a letter?"

Mitchell sighed, giving her a sad smile. "He's here, Allie."

Her stomach nose-dived. "Where?" She turned, scanning the ballroom to make sure her mother was all right.

"Not at the wedding, sweetheart. In the hotel. I found out this morning."

"And you didn't tell me?" she whispered, raising her focus to meet his concerned gaze.

He shook his head. "No. I didn't want to worry you. But that was the reason for the increase in security. He wanted to see you today and wouldn't take no for an answer." A calloused hand grabbed hers, entwining their fingers. "Did I make the right decision?"

"Yes." She nodded. There was no doubt. No need to consider. Alana couldn't bear to think what would've happened if her parents were placed

SULTRY GROOVE

in the same room together. Her mother wasn't ready for that. "I still don't understand, though. Why is he here?"

"I assume the letter will explain."

Alana stared at the weight that grew heavier in her hand, unsure whether to open it, especially tonight. Since she was a little girl, she'd longed for a father. Not just someone to play catch with her, or tell her how beautiful she was, she yearned for the love only a dad could give. The tiny piece of her that had always been missing. She wanted a man to care for her and her mother. Anyone except the man she'd grown up loathing.

Yet her grandparents had spoken of a kind-hearted soul. One who cared for her from afar. A normal guy who made a monumental mistake he hadn't stopped paying for. Time had given her the confidence to decide she could never love a man capable of hurting her mother, but being able to understand him would be nice.

"Do you think I should open it?" she asked. Pressure built in her chest. She needed to read what was inside the letter. But would the contents ruin their night?

"I can't answer that, Allie." Mitchell spoke low, the sorrow heavy in his voice. "I can deal with whatever is in there. I'm just not sure if you can."

She wasn't sure either, and there was only one way to find out. With an increasing heartbeat, she opened the envelope, convincing herself she could stop at any moment. Then the letter was unfolded in her shaking hands, the neat script staring back at her, and it was too late to turn back.

Dearest Alana,

I wanted you to know I was here. That your father was thinking of you on your wedding day. Although I've never been a part of your life, you have always meant everything to me. And I hope, with your mother and Mitchell's blessing, that in the future, we can get to know one another.

I've made mistakes. We all know that. And I've suffered every day because of them. But none more so than today—the day

134

my daughter got married. I wish you both all the happiness in the world. I wish you luck, and success, and love, but most of all I wish upon you the ability to forgive.

With love,

Chris Bowen.

Her eyes burned, the slow trail of tears flowing down her cheeks to hit the paper.

"You OK, sweetheart?" Mitchell's hands stroked her upper arms, wiping away the frigid cold in her chest.

"I think so." She was shaking, her hands, her arms, her legs. She re-read the letter, her heart clenching a little more this time.

"I have his room number if you want to see him."

Did she want that? Her gaze sought her mother again. The soft glow from the table candles illuminated her happiness. Finally, after years of living with a haunted past, she was starting to let go. To be free from the fear that overtook her for so long.

"No." Alana shook her head, carefully placing the letter back into the envelope. "Not tonight." She stepped into Mitchell, wrapping her arms around his waist and brushed her lips against his. "Today has been perfect. I married the man I adore. My mom is finally losing some of the craziness we've all grown to fear. And my father..." she shrugged, "loves me."

Never in her wildest dreams could her wedding day be so fulfilling.

"You're a strong woman, Alana."

No. She wasn't strong. She gained her strength from the people who supported her—Mitchell, her mother, the Reckless Beat crew. Having them behind her made everything easier, she only hoped Blake and Gabi felt the same with their struggles.

"I'm strong because you love me."

"And I always will." He kissed her, his tongue breaching her mouth with a delicate sweep. They swayed to the music, their passion heating with every brush of their lips.

"Why don't we say goodbye to our guests and head to the penthouse?"

she asked.

He rested his head against hers and tilted the hardness of his erection into her abdomen. "How about we skip the formalities? I can't wait that long."

She chuckled against his lips, her core already clenching at the thought of alone time. He took her hand and stepped back, leading her around the darkened edge of the ballroom, to escape unnoticed.

It was the end of a brilliant day, and only the start of a beautiful life together.

EPILOGUE

"**T**IME TO GET LAID, BROTHER." MASON PUSHED FROM HIS CHAIR, LESS THAN enthusiastic about the prospect as he patted Sean on the back. "I'll catch you later."

He was in the mood for a leggy blonde. Or a redhead. Maybe both, if they were lucky.

"Who are you taking home tonight?" Ryan slurred and slumped forward in his chair. The poor guy was drowning his Oompa Loompa sorrows, and Mason didn't have the heart to ask why. He wasn't good with marital issues. They all knew he'd never had a long-term relationship.

"Not sure, buddy, but maybe your next drink should be water."

"Water?" Ryan frowned. "I don't get you," he raised his voice, waving a drunken finger in Mason's direction. "Ninety-nine, point fuckin' nine, nine, nine, nine percent of the time you are a *dick*. A *big* dick. Then you tell me to drink some water and I fall in love wiff you all over again."

Ryan's head fell back, and for a moment Mason grinned, thinking the poor guy had passed out. Then the guitarist swung forward, teetering in an upright position. "Why'd you do that?" he asked, his eyes still closed. "Why are you a dick? Then not a dick?"

Mason ignored the question as his smile faded. He had no control over the asshole he'd become. He didn't like it, yet this was who he was now. The music industry had made him into a skeptical, heartless prick, and he'd resigned himself to the lifestyle. Some people had love and happiness and friendships that didn't end in backstabbing and deceit. Others had fame and fortune and the nastiness that followed. Nobody got it all. And he sure as shit wasn't going to cry a river over the hand he'd been dealt. His cards were still fucking brilliant.

"Sean, get him some water, would ya?" Mason had lived through enough A-grade hangovers to know Ryan didn't need one right now.

"Yeah. No problem." Sean nodded and pushed from his chair. "Have fun."

Mason gave a two-finger salute and strode off to find the bride and groom. He skirted the dance floor, keeping his gaze away from Alana's vulture of a friend, Kate. The woman didn't have a subtle bone in her body, and there was no way she was getting his tonight.

"Ahh, just the man I wanted to see." Leah's voice sent a shiver down his spine.

He hated that she now made him nervous. He didn't *do* nervous. Never had...until recently.

"Hello, Leah," he drawled, not making eye contact. "I'm about to say goodbye to the happy couple and call it a night."

"They already left. Good decision though, you need all the sleep you can get."

A pulse ticked to life under his right eye. "Don't start." He narrowed his gaze on her, backing up his demand with the visual threat. He didn't want to start a fight in the middle of a wedding.

"I'm not starting anything."

Yeah, she was. She'd been hassling him for months, her phone calls and emails becoming more frequent and demanding. The looming pressure was becoming too much. He no longer had the drive to create a new album. Or go on tour for fans who loved Reckless one minute, then fucked them over on every social media outlet the next. All he had to do was miss a note, or have Sean fumble a beat, or Mitch fuck up a chord. Then the claws came out and the nastiness began. Everyone was a critic. Loyalty was a thing of the past.

The more he thought about it, the more it pissed him off.

He couldn't even trust his relatives anymore. They didn't give a shit about his life. They cared about free concert tickets and the popularity that filtered through the family tree. Yet they only stuck around during the good days. If a scandal broke, or bad publicity spanned the headlines, his uncles would be straight on the phone to his mom, bitching and complaining about how it affected their lives. *His* life, and the lives of his bandmates, were nobody's fucking business.

"I told you I'd back off for tonight," Leah continued. "I'm here as a guest, not as your band manager."

Well then, lay the hell off. Constantly bugging him about a muse he had no control over wouldn't help kick-start the next album. "Good night, then." He'd had enough. He was drained, tired in body and mind, and for once he wanted peace. He wanted to go home alone and not scrutinize himself on the reasons behind his songwriting issues.

"I'll give you a week," Leah added. "After that, I'm going to ride you so hard your ass bleeds." Her face broke out in a dazzling smile. "And it might be the alcohol talking, but I'm kinda looking forward to it."

He clenched his jaw and fought hard to bite back the anger poised at his tongue. He hated this. Hated being unable to do his job. Hated that his muse had packed up and gone on a vacation with no end in sight. Most of all he hated being weak. He was the front man and songwriter for one of the bestselling rock bands in the world—he didn't do weak. He *did* loud and proud and fucking awesome.

"Fuck it, Leah." He threw his arms up in the air, unconcerned by the way she jerked back. "I quit."

The label could find another sucker to earn them billions. He'd started on the music path with stars in his eyes and music the solitary focus in his heart. Now he was a monster, and worst of all, he'd become used to the constant criticism. No wonder his muse was dead and buried, how could he write when he hated himself?

The humor fled Leah's features. "Mason, get a grip. I was joking."

"Well, I wasn't."

He was walking away. Taking a break. Giving himself time to consider the different paths on offer because he was fed up with the road he was on.

There were too many rules. Too many fucked up issues that manipulated the heart of his music. All their songs had to stick to a similar style. They couldn't deviate. They couldn't test the waters with other genres or sounds.

He was sick of creating lyrics to match current trends. He wanted to write from the heart, if he ever found his again. Most of all he wanted to be free to do whatever the hell he liked.

Enough. Christ, he was rambling to himself.

"Mason?" Leah uttered.

"Call the label. Tell them I'm stepping away from my contract." He breathed deep through his nose, ignoring the panic in Leah's eyes. "I can't do this shit anymore."

Without another word, he turned and strode from the ballroom, unsure whether the hard throb behind his breastbone was from relief, or fear of making the biggest mistake of his life.

PLEASE CONSIDER LEAVING A REVIEW ON YOUR BOOK RETAILER WEBSITE OR GOODREADS

LOOK FOR THESE TITLES FROM EDEN SUMMERS

RECKLESS BEAT SERIES

Blind Attraction (Reckless Beat #1)
Passionate Addiction (Reckless Beat #2)
Reckless Weekend (Reckless Beat #2.5)
Undesired Lust (Reckless Beat #3)
Sultry Groove (Reckless Beat #4)
Reckless Rendezvous (Reckless Beat #4.5)

VAULT OF SIN SERIES

A Shot of Sin (Vault of Sin #1)
Union of Sin (Vault of Sin #2)

STANDALONE SERIES

Concealed Desire
Sneaking a Peek
"Phantom Pleasure" Halloween Heat V

KEEP READING FOR A
SNEAK PEEK OF

Undesired Lust

One

TWO YEARS AGO

*"**A**ND THE GRAMMY FOR BEST ROCK SONG GOES TO...**"***

Sidney Higgins held her breath, her gaze glued to the presenter aglow in stage lights. Mason Lynch sat to her left, his hand holding hers in a reassuring grip. Tonight, he was more gorgeous than usual, in a tailored black suit and his blond, wavy hair loose against his jaw line. She didn't need to glance his way to know his confident smile was aimed at her. She could feel it on her skin, the light tingle of awareness which always haunted her whenever he was close.

"Don't sweat it. We've got this in the bag," he murmured over the hush in the room.

His arrogance never ceased to amaze her. It was natural to him. Effortless. Strangely, she found it endearing. His confidence rubbed off on her, increasing her sense of accomplishment, not only in her career, but life in general.

Right now, though, his sonic boom of awesomeness wasn't penetrating her nerves, or her need to use the bathroom. This was her first Grammy nomination, and the butterflies alone were enough to make her double over.

"... Mason Lynch and Sidney Higgins for 'Tough Love.'"

Oh my god.

They did it. They won a fucking Grammy.

"I don't believe it." The words tightened her throat, whispering from her lips as thunderous applause erupted around them. She turned her wide-eyed gaze to Mason and found him staring at her, grinning. No elation. No shock or disbelief. He simply stared at her as if the sun rose and set in her eyes.

Someone clapped her shoulder, followed by another and another. She was too awe struck and numb to notice who. Her focus was glued to the gleaming, mocha-brown irises of the most talented man she'd ever known. He stood, continuing to hold her hand and her attention as he tugged her to her feet.

"Let's get you a Grammy, kitten."

Ovaries—boom. That endearment did it to her every time. Her nipples hardened. And right now, in a skintight evening gown and thin lace bra, she couldn't think of anything worse. *Think of dirty dishes, laundry, clubbing baby seals.* Hell, even the thought of the unsigned recording contract currently sitting on her dining room table wasn't enough to drag her mind from lurid thoughts of Mason.

Clearing the gravel from her throat, she followed him into the aisle leading to the stage, and sneaked a glance over her shoulder at the hundreds of applauding people. *Surreal.* The man of her dreams at her side. A Grammy waiting to be awarded. The world at her feet. Tears stung her eyes, and her grin turned into a beaming smile. Everything fell into place. Life was perfect, and maybe this achievement would stop her father from worrying about her risky career choice.

Mason tugged her into his arms and then squeezed her tight, placing a gentle kiss on her cheek. "Congratulations, Sid," he whispered against her neck, sending a shiver of awareness down her spine.

She hugged him, her pulse pounding in her ears. "We really did it."

"You doubted our unstoppable skills? The world doesn't stand a chance against us." He pulled back, gifting her with another delicate sweep of his lips, this time on her temple. "Now let's go get our prize."

•••

Mason reclined into the rooftop sofa, scotch in hand, and stared at the woman dancing with his best friend, Sean. *Perfection.* That was the only way to describe her. Her sweet, lush lips, her playful, hazel eyes, the way her hips swayed as she twirled in those sexy little heels. He had a thing for her. Maybe not a big thing, but it was definitely growing if the crotch of his pants was anything to go by.

Sean caught his gaze and waggled his brows. "I'm dancing with a Grammy award winner!" His voice died under the beat of techno crap the *dick* jockey was playing. They were at a Grammy after party for fuck's sake. *Play some good music, asshole.*

"You can blow one, if you like," Mason shouted.

Sidney burst into laughter, her head falling back, the short, almost-black hair fanning her shoulders as she clung to Sean's biceps. When she straightened, her dimples hit Mason with the force of a truck driver on speed. He could watch her for hours, had already done so while working together on the latest Reckless Beat album. He didn't think his libido would ever get enough.

Jutting his chin, he commanded her in a not-so-subtle way to get her sexy ass to his side. Her brow quirked in response while she continued to dance, making her moves more sultry. More fucking hard to ignore. And he'd been such a good boy until now. He'd made sure all their collaboration time had been purely platonic, even though he had to battle lust daily. He'd matched her high level of professionalism, played it cool, and instead of pushing her up against the nearest studio wall and fucking her senseless, he'd waited until he was alone to shoot his enthusiasm all over the shower wall like a pubescent teen.

Yep. She was that fucking brilliant. And he couldn't turn his fantasies into reality because they worked together. The risks were too high. Sidney was the only person he'd successfully collaborated with. She got him. They shared the same musical spirit, and he knew their relationship would be compromised if he got her hot little body beneath his. Well, he *had* known when the shit flowing through his veins wasn't eighty percent alcohol.

Right now, she looked like a challenge he wanted to accomplish. More than once.

"Come on." He jerked his head again and crooked a finger. *Don't play hard to get. It drives me fucking wild.*

She paused, her dance moves slowing as she scraped her lower lip between her teeth.

Yeah, that's it, little kitten. Come to papa.

His heart stopped with the first step she took in his direction. Then the fucker restarted in double-time. She prowled toward him, her normally professional demeanor nowhere in sight. He'd been used to Sidney Higgins—business woman and songwriter extraordinaire. The female—this stranger—sashaying toward him was a seductress, and entirely in control of his libido.

She stopped in front of him, the tips of her shoes touching his. "You summoned me?"

He gulped the final swig of his scotch, hoping the burn would take the edge off his arousal. His dick twitched against his thigh. Nope. No luck there. His mic was still wired for sound. "Want to go someplace quiet?"

In an instant, the seductress vanished and her wide-eyed stare made him doubt his question.

"Where we goin'?" Sean interrupted, coming up behind Sidney and placing his chin on her shoulder.

"Back to my hotel room. I've got the penthouse. Stocked bar. Room service. We can take our shoes off, put on real music, and celebrate our achievement in style."

"Sounds good to me." Sean tilted his head, his lips hovering close to Sidney's ear. "What do you say, award winning songstress?"

Mason wanted to kick his friend in the balls, but violence wouldn't work in his favor. Besides, Sean could be a buffer. A third wheel would make Sidney more comfortable. Then again, having Sean unable to use his junk might be a valuable strategy.

She let out a half-hearted chuckle, her gaze still nervously holding Mason's. "I guess so. I won't stay long, though. We passed my bedtime hours ago."

"We can go straight to bed if you like." The line flew from his lips before he could hold the fucker in.

Sidney's eyes narrowed, scrutinizing him, leaving nothing but the heavy techno beat hammering between them. He didn't mind, he loved the attention, always had. Even better was the enticing swipe of her tongue gliding along her grinning lips.

"Don't get yourself in trouble, Mason. I'm not always a little kitten."

ABOUT THE AUTHOR

Eden Summers is a true blue Aussie, living in regional New South Wales with her two energetic young boys and a quick witted husband.

In late 2010, Eden's romance obsession could no longer be sated by reading alone, so she decided to give voice to the sexy men and sassy women in her mind.

Eden can't resist alpha dominance, dark features and sarcasm in her fictional heroes and loves a strong heroins who knows when to bite her tongue but also serves retribution with a feminine smile on her face.

W: www.edensummers.com

E: eden@edensummers.com

F: www.facebook.com/authoredensummers

T: twitter.com/EdenSummers1

52439106R00095

Made in the USA
Columbia, SC
03 March 2019